THE P.K. PINKERTON MYSTERIES

The Case of the Deadly Desperados

Caroline Lawrence

Orion
Children's Books

First published in Great Britain in 2011
by Orion Children's Books
This edition first published in 2012
by Orion Children's Books
a division of the Orion Publishing Group Ltd
Orion House
5 Upper St Martin's Lane
London WC2H 9EA
An Hachette UK company

1 3 5 7 9 10 8 6 4 2

A catalogue record for this book
is available from the British Library.

ISBN 978 1 4440 0325 3

Printed in Great Britain by Clays Ltd, St Ives plc

To my friend Penny, who started me on this dusty trail when she gave me a copy of *True Grit* by Charles Portis

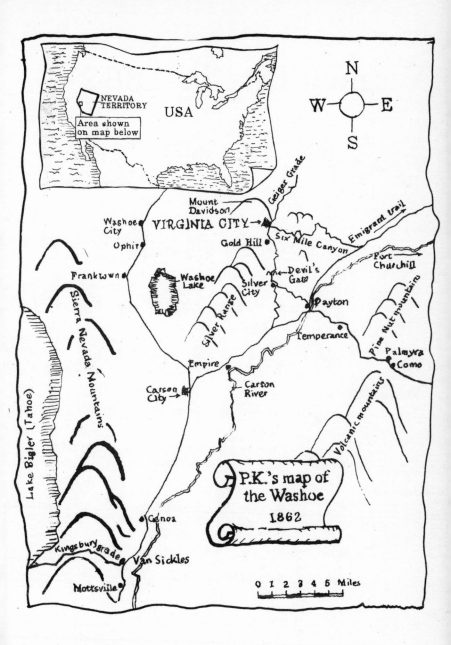

Virginia City in 1862

LEDGER SHEET 1

MY NAME IS **P.K. P**INKERTON AND BEFORE THIS day is over I will be dead.

I am trapped down the deepest shaft of a Comstock silver mine with three desperados closing in on me.

Until they find me, I have my pencil & these ledger sheets and a couple of candles. If I write small & fast, I might be able to write an account of how I came to be here. Then whoever finds my body will know the unhappy events that led to my demise.

And they will also know who done it.

This is what I would like my tombstone to say:

P.K. PINKERTON

BORN IN HARD LUCK, SEPTEMBER 26, 1850

DIED IN VIRGINIA CITY, SEPTEMBER 28, 1862

'YE ARE ALL ONE IN CHRIST JESUS' GALATIANS 3:28

R.I.P.

My foster ma Evangeline used to say that when God gives you a Gift he always gives you a Thorn in your side to keep you humble.

My Gift is that I am real smart about certain things.

I can read & write and do any sum in my head. I can speak American & Lakota and also some Chinese & Spanish. I can shoot a gun & I can ride a pony with or without a saddle. I can track & shoot & skin any game and then cook it over a self-sparked fire. I know how to cure a headache with a handful of weeds.

I can hear a baby quail in the sage-brush or a mouse in the pantry.

I can tell what a horse has been eating just by the smell of his manure.

I can see every leaf on a cottonwood tree.

But here is my Problem: I cannot tell if a person's smile is genuine or false. I can only spot three emotions: happiness, fear & anger. And sometimes I even mix those up.

Also, sometimes I do not recognize someone I have met before. If they have grown a beard or their hair is different then I get confused.

That is my Thorn: people confound me.

And now my Thorn has got me killed.

LEDGER SHEET 2

IT ALL STARTED THE DAY BEFORE YESTERDAY, ON September 26th. I came home from school & walked into our one-room cabin to the smell of scalded milk & the sight of things thrown everywhere. I closed the door behind me & stepped forward. It was only then that I saw my foster parents lying on the floor in a pool of blood.

They had both been scalped & they appeared to be dead.

I ran to ma first. She was holding the big iron skillet and it had some hair & blood on it so I guessed she had put up a fight.

As I stood there looking down, her eyelids fluttered and she opened her eyes and said 'Pinky?' Pinky was her nickname for me. It is short for Pinkerton.

I crouched down beside her. 'I'm here, Ma.'

She said, 'Is Emmet alive?'

I looked over at pa. He was not breathing. His eyes

were closed & he had a peaceful smile on his face. He also had a hatchet buried in his chest. I swallowed hard.

'No, Ma,' I said.

'He was a good man,' she said. 'I will see him walking the Streets of Glory before too long.'

'Don't talk that way, Ma. I will fetch Doc Finley from Dayton.'

'No.' Her voice was faint. 'There is no time. I'm dying. Your medicine bag. The one your other ma gave you.'

'I do not think my medicine bag can help you now, Ma.'

'No. I mean…that's what they were after.' She gave a kind of sigh and I thought she had gone. But then her eyes opened & she gripped my hand tight. 'It holds your Destiny. Pinky, do you remember my special hiding place?'

'Loose floorboard behind the stove?'

She nodded. 'You're smart, Pinky. You'll figure out what to do. Take that medicine bag and get out fast. Before they come back.'

I did not understand what she meant at first. Then I did. 'The Indians who did this might come back?' I said.

'They weren't Indians.' Her voice was real faint now & her skin was a terrible white. She said, 'One of them had blue eyes. And he smelled like Bay Rum Hair Tonic. Indians do not wear Hair Tonic.'

I sniffed the air. Ma Evangeline was right. Above the smell of blood, scalded milk & fresh-baked cake, I could detect the sweet scent of cloves: Bay Rum Hair Tonic. I also picked up a tang of sweaty armpits.

The men who did this had left a few minutes ago & could return any moment. My instinct was to run, but I did not want to leave my dying ma.

'Go, Pinky,' she said. 'Take your medicine bag and get out of here before they come back.'

I stood up & looked down at her. She would be dead in a minute. I clenched my fists.

'I will find those men,' I said. 'And I will avenge you, Ma.'

'No,' she said. And then she said, 'Pinky?'

I could barely hear her so I squatted down beside her again. 'Yes, Ma?'

'Promise me you that you will never take another life. Not even those who killed me. You must forgive. That is what our Lord teaches.'

'I can't promise that, Ma,' I said. My vision was blurry. I blinked & it got clearer.

'It is my dying wish,' she said. 'You have to.'

'Then I promise,' I said.

She closed her eyes & whispered, 'And promise you will not gamble nor drink hard liquor.'

'I promise.'

But this time she did not hear me.

I stood & looked down at the bodies of my foster ma & pa. They lay next to each other and the pool of mingled blood was still spreading.

I went over to the stove, carefully picking my way around the things that had been thrown down. A tin

5

canister of flour had been emptied onto the floor. I made sure I stepped around it. Flour would make me leave footprints as sure as blood.

I took the burning milk off the hotplate. Then I knelt down beside the stove & felt for the floorboard with the little knothole. I got my fingertip in there & pulled it up. I found my medicine bag & took it out. I hung it around my neck. I also found a gold coin worth $20 that ma kept for emergencies. She would not need it now, so I took that, too. I put it in my medicine bag with the other things. Then I put the board back in its place.

Outside I heard men speaking in hushed tones. One of the porch stairs creaked.

I knew it was them. The killers were coming back.

I looked around the house. There were not a lot of places in that one-roomed cabin that I could hide.

It seemed to me there was only one.

LEDGER SHEET 3

OVER AGAINST THE FAR WALL OF THE CABIN STOOD
Ma Evangeline's tall pine dresser. Its shelves were about
half full of books and half full of plates.

I scrambled up that dresser as fast as a squirrel with
its tail on fire. When I got near the top I half turned and
leapt onto one of the two big rafters of the house. I am
small for my age, but I am agile.

I was up on the rafter before the door handle even
began to turn, but in my haste I had set some of the
china trembling. As the front door eased open I noticed a
big blue & white plate rolling along the top of the dresser.

It slowed, hesitated, and then stopped right at the
edge.

I breathed a sigh of relief, then froze as I heard a
man's whiny voice say, 'Is it safe?'

'Yeah it's safe,' said a deeper voice. 'They's still dead.
Come on you big scaredy-cat.'

'I ain't a scaredy-cat,' said the one with the whiny voice. 'That woman brained me real good with the skillet. It hurt.'

I peeped over the edge of the big rafter and saw three men below me. They sounded like white men but they looked like Indians. Then I looked closer and saw they were white men dressed up as Indians. They were wearing canvas pantaloons, not buckskins, and their moccasins were clumsy things made of buffalo hide. They had war paint on their faces & turkey feathers in their greasy hair. One of the men smelled strongly of Bay Rum Hair Tonic. From up above I could not be sure which one was wearing the Hair Tonic but I guessed it was the man with three turkey feathers. He was leading the others across the room.

I held onto the roof beam & tried a trick my Indian ma had once told me about. It is called The Bush Trick. If you hide behind a small bush and imagine that you are that bush, they say you become invisible. I did The Beam Trick. I pretended I was part of that beam. I concentrated real hard & prayed my Indian ma had been right.

'I told you they wouldn't of hid it in the outhouse,' I heard the leader say. 'And now they're dead. We won't get no more out of them.' He went over to my pa, looked down at him & said, *'Nothin can happen more beautiful than death.'* Then he laughed & took the hatchet by the handle & tugged. It made a sucking noise as it came out.

'Let's get out of here, Walt,' said Whiny Voice. 'I don't feel so good.'

'Yeah, Walt,' said the third man. He was tall & had a raspy voice. 'Whatever you're looking for, it ain't here.'

'Dang,' Walt said. (Only he used the bad word that starts with D and ends with MN.) He spat some tobacco-tinted saliva onto the floor. 'It's gotta be here. I just ain't figured out where.' There was a pause and in that moment of silence I thought they must surely hear my heart thumping. Then Walt said, 'Well lookee here.'

I squirmed forward a little & looked down and saw what I had not noticed before. On the table was a cake with chocolate frosting & red licorice strings on top that spelled out: HAPPY 12ᵀᴴ BIRTHDAY PINKY. It was a layer cake: my favorite. It must have cost Ma Evangeline a fortune to get chocolate out here in the Nevada desert.

'They got a kid?' said Whiny Voice. From up here I could see the bloody patch on his head from where ma had hit him with the skillet.

'Course they got a kid, you fool,' said Walt. 'Kid's real ma was the one who had what we are looking for.'

'Maybe the kid has it,' said Raspy Voice.

'Pinky a girl's name or a boy's?' said Whiny Voice.

'Boy's name,' said Raspy. 'I knew a Pinky in Hangtown. Pinky O'Malley. He was one of them Albino types. White hair and pink eyes.'

'What about Pinky's Saloon in Esmeralda?' said Whiny. 'That's owned by a lady. A French lady, I think.'

Walt had taken out a fearsome Bowie Knife and was cutting himself a chaw from a plug of tobacco. He said, 'Shut your traps, you two. I am trying to think.' He ate the tobacco right off that blade & chomped for a while. Then he said, 'Is there a school in this flea-bitten excuse for a town?'

'Dayton,' said Raspy. 'I think there's a schoolhouse down in Dayton. But I saw some kids over by the church when we rode up earlier.'

'Let's check it out,' said Walt. 'We gotta find that kid.' He started towards the door & I was about to breathe a sigh of relief. Then he stopped & turned slowly back to the stove. 'Wait a minute,' he said. 'I reckon someone has been here since we kilt Mr. & Mrs. Preacher.'

'What do you mean, Walt?' Whiny Voice touched the bloody place on his head & brought his hand away fast.

'Something here is different,' said Walt. 'Somebody has taken the milk off the heat. And I'll bet they are still here.'

As **W**alt **looked around for the person who** had taken the milk off the stove, I closed my eyes & held my breath. I pretended to be part of the rafter. The blood was leaping in my veins.

I heard Whiny Voice say, 'I think that might of been me, Walt.'

'You sure?'

'Yeah,' Whiny Voice said. He sounded nervous. 'Ain't nobody here, Walt. Let's skedaddle. Townspeople will lynch us if they find us dressed like Injuns with their dead scalped preacher & his wife.'

Walt spat again. 'Flyspeck town like this, I reckon we outnumber the townspeople. And we gotta find that kid. Let's try the church.'

I heard their footsteps going out but I did not hear the door close. After a while I opened my eyes. After a while longer I wormed my way along the rafter to the wall &

used the window frame to climb down from my hiding place.

Walt was right. Temperance is a flyspeck of a town here in the Nevada Territory. It is on scrubland at the foot of the Pine Nut Mountains, between Palmyra & Dayton. Apart from our cabin & a few one-room wooden frame houses, there is a dry goods store, a livery stable & a small church with a half-built steeple. There is no saloon & no place to buy whiskey, so the name Temperance is fitting.

The Rev. Emmet Jones, my foster father, founded this town after a day of prayer & fasting. He said he would build a town where there was nothing to tempt a person to sin. He said it would make his job easier. That shows you how little he knew about human nature. He is probably being lowered into his coffin as I write this, with a hatchet-shaped hole in his chest.

My pa hoped Temperance would be an Oasis of Holiness in a Desert of Sin. But Temperance is not an oasis. It is a failure. The stagecoach only stops there if someone is standing in the middle of the road waving. And it usually only stops if there is room on board, or if the person flagging the lift is either pretty or rich. It is two miles to Dayton, and from there the stage goes up the Toll Road to Virginia City & all those big moneymaking silver mines on the Comstock Lode.

The 4 oclock stage was due any minute and one way or another I wanted to be on it.

I had to get out of Temperance fast.

When I snuck out of the house that day, the day my foster parents were killed, the first place I ran to was the privy. I hoped Walt & his men would not be anywhere near there, because I needed it real bad. After I did my business, I came out at a crouch & threw myself down on the dust. I wormed my way from sage-brush to sage-brush, heading for the western end of town. With only half a dozen buildings that did not take me long.

Usually you have to wear itchy black trowsers & a starched white shirt & heavy boots to school, but because it was my birthday ma had let me wear my new attire, a set of butter-soft fringed buckskins that she had sewed herself. They were a pale gold color so I blended in real good as I crawled through the dust. I was heading towards a big clump of sage-brush by the road.

When I got there I smelled a bad smell and saw a dead coyote with flies buzzing around it. I recoiled when I saw it & thought of moving on. But that bush was the only cover around, and it was nearly time for the 4 oclock stagecoach. I shoved the coyote corpse under the bush with my elbow & lay there on my stomach with my heart pounding & feeling kind of sick.

Then I prayed.

When I lifted my head again, I noticed there were two horses & a mule standing behind Gould's Dry Goods. I had never seen them before. The horses were a blue roan gelding & a bay mare. The big mule was a dirty white color.

I thought, 'Those must be Walt's mounts.'

I also thought, 'When is that stagecoach coming?'

And finally, 'What could be in my medicine bag worth dying for?'

I pushed myself up on my elbows, pulled the medicine bag out from the neck of my buckskin shirt. It was made of buffalo hide & decorated with red & blue beads in a little arrow shape. It was as big as my right hand with the fingers spread out. My Indian ma had given it to me before we set out on the wagon train West. I had been wearing it around my neck during the massacre but I had not seen it since my foster parents put it in the hiding place under the floorboard. I thought I remembered what was in it but I wanted to make sure, so I opened the flap and spilled out the contents onto the dirt. Apart from the $20 gold coin, there were three things in there: my Indian ma's flint knife, a piece of folded paper, & a brass button that belonged to my original pa.

My original pa was named Robert Pinkerton. He was around a while after I was born but he went off to be a Rail Road Detective and never came back. I was seven when my ma got word that he had died defending a train against robbers. But I had not seen him since I was about two and I do not remember him. The only thing he left me was that brass button off his jacket. She told me it fell off his jacket the day they met & she had always meant to sew it back on but had never got around to it.

My Christian ma Evangeline loved Detective Stories & Dime Novels. When she & pa Emmet first took me in & I told them my original pa was Robert Pinkerton, a Rail Road Detective, she got real excited. She said my pa's brother was probably Allan Pinkerton, who had established a famous Detective Agency in Chicago & coined the phrase 'Private Eye'. That made him my uncle.

She told me a Detective is someone who uncovers the Truth & brings Justice.

She told me a Rail Road Detective is someone who defends passengers & goods from bandits.

She told me Allan Pinkerton was a champion of the Negro & that he employed Lady Detectives as well as men & she said a Free Thinker like Allan Pinkerton might be glad to have news of me.

So Ma Evangeline wrote to Allan Pinkerton in Chicago, to ask him if his dead brother had ever fathered a child by a Lakota squaw around the year 1850. We waited eagerly for a reply, but we never got one. We were living near Salt Lake City in Utah Territory then.

Last year, when the newspapers told how my famous uncle saved Abraham Lincoln from an assassination attempt, she wrote to him again, asking if he knew about me. But then we set out for the Nevada Territory. If he sent a reply, it never found us.

Lying there in the hot dust by that sage-brush, I held my dead pa's button in my hand for the first time in two years. Now that I could read, I saw the small button had writing on it. Curved around the top was the name PINKERTON. Curved around the bottom it said RAIL ROAD. And right across the middle it said DETECTIVE.

I slipped the button into my pocket. It meant a lot to me, but I doubted it was what Walt & his gang were after.

The flint knife was good for skinning rabbits, but you could get a flint knife anywhere. Sometimes you could pick them right up off the ground.

I reckoned it was the piece of paper they were after.

I remembered it had been in my Indian ma's medicine bag when she gave it to me, but of course I could not read then.

I unfolded the piece of paper & examined it.

It was a Letter addressed 'To Whom it May Concern'. It promised 'The Bearer' several acres near Pleasant Town on Sun Peak, between the Divide & the Creek, & also 'the stone cabin on Grizzly Hill & all the goods therein'. It was signed by E. A. Somebody. The surname was a scrawl. It might have started with an 'O' or a 'G' or even a 'D'. I did not know where Pleasant Town was, or to which Divide or Creek it referred.

Then I saw the signature of the witness. It was signed Rbt. Pinkerton and it was dated Nov 21, 1857. I had just turned seven at the time he witnessed the Letter, but I had not seen him for years. I reckon he must have been killed shortly after he witnessed this Letter because we had word of his death that Christmas.

I folded the paper carefully & put it back in my medicine bag along with my ma's knife & the $20 coin, but I kept the Button in my pocket.

I figured the stagecoach was due any moment. I pressed my ear to the dirt & heard the faint rumble of horses' hooves coming in the distance.

I thought, 'If I can just stay invisible for a few more minutes I will be safe.'

I tried The Bush Trick.

But it was hard to pretend to be a sage bush because the dead coyote kept reminding me of my dead ma & pa.

Something else was bothering me, too.

It was that prickly feeling I sometimes get when I am being watched.

Then I heard a voice yell, 'There he is! Get him, boys!'

LEDGER SHEET 5

I WAS UP **&** RUNNING AS FAST AS A JACKRABBIT, but then someone tackled me & I went down hard. All the air burst out of my lungs & I got a mouthful of dirt. I spat it out. My attacker rolled me over & sat on top of me.

I was relieved to see it was only Olaf, one of the three school bullies. All three lived in Temperance & all three were as mean as skunks, but Olaf was the worst. He nodded to his pardners. Abe put a foot on my left wrist and Charlie stamped down on my right. They were not wearing soft moccasins like me. They were wearing heavy school shoes.

'Why were you running away from us?' said Olaf in a pleasant tone of voice. He was sitting on me & I could hardly breathe. 'You didn't think we would beat on you today, did you? Ain't it your birthday?'

I nodded.

Olaf stood up and looked at Abe & Charlie. 'Shall we give him a birthday present?'

'Yeah,' said the other two. They took their feet off my wrists.

'Do you like punch, P.K.?' Olaf was smiling.

I am not good at reading people.

Ma Evangeline told me you had to look at a person's face real careful to know what they are thinking. She taught me five Expressions to look out for.

1. If someone's mouth curves up & their eyes crinkle, that is a Genuine Smile.
2. If their mouth stretches sideways & their eyes are not crinkled, that is a Fake Smile.
3. If a person turns down their mouth & crinkles up their nose, they are disgusted.
4. If their eyes open real wide, they are probably surprised or scared.
5. If they make their eyes narrow, they are either mad at you or thinking or suspicious.

I was pretty sure Olaf was giving me Expression No. 2, the Fake Smile. But the sun was right behind his head & there was dust in my eye & I could not see his face clearly enough to tell.

'Do you like punch?' he said again.

I like punch more than getting beat up. So I nodded, even though I was pretty sure it was a trick question.

I was right. It was a trick question.

Olaf looked at the other two. 'Let's give this Freak of Nature twelve punches,' he said. 'One for each year. Ha, ha, ha.'

They bent over & started punching me so I curled up like a woodlouse.

All of a sudden they stopped beating on me & Olaf said, 'Look. The rest of his filthy tribe is coming to save him.'

'Those don't look like no Injuns I ever seen,' said Abe.

'Does that one in front have blood on his tomahawk?' asked Charlie. His voice was kind of wobbly.

'Are those scalps hanging off his belt?' Abe's voice cracked.

I unsquinched my eyes & turned my head to see where he was looking.

Walt & his two fake Indian friends were coming down the road on foot. Walt was holding the hatchet that had been buried in my pa's chest. It was still bloody. They were heading straight towards us with purpose & intent.

'Dang!' cried Olaf. He eyes went real wide. He was either surprised or scared, or maybe both. 'Let's skedaddle!'

He & the others ran off towards some scrub pines about half a mile distant. I do not think that was very clever. If you meet a bear & you skedaddle, he will run after you. Sure enough, as soon as they started running, Walt & his gang tore after them. One of Walt's men pulled out a pistol & started firing. It was a Colt's Navy Revolver from the sound of it. This made my schoolmates run even faster. I could hear them yelping like coyotes pursued by a bear.

For some reason Walt & his gang had not noticed me. Wearing my buckskins, I reckon I looked like a little bump on the ground. Also, I think they were too busy chasing Olaf, Charlie & Abe. Those three boys were wearing their black pants & white shirts and they stood out real good against the pale desert.

Meanwhile, the stagecoach had appeared. It was rumbling through town & raising a plume of yellow dust behind it.

I knew it would not stop for a muddy-skinned, buckskin-clad kid like me.

That suited me just fine.

I did not want it to stop in case Walt & his pals noticed.

I just needed it to slow down.

I scrambled back to the sage-brush, pulled out the dead coyote by one of its stiff hind legs & nudged it out into the road so that it would be in the direct path of the horses. It was about the same color as the dirt road and I hoped that meant the driver would not notice it too soon.

Horses do not like to trample on things. Even the best driver cannot easily make them run over a person or animal in their path. This driver was a good one. When he saw the stiff coyote in the road, he tugged on the reins to slow his team & to steer them around the dead coyote. The coach passed close by my bush & before it could pick up speed again I leapt out & jumped up onto the mail boot on the back.

I clung on like a tick to a dog and prayed Walt and his pards would not notice me.

LEDGER SHEET 6

AT THE BACK OF THE STAGECOACH WAS A BIG
leather pouch for mail along with some canvas straps
for extra luggage. I clung onto the straps for a while
and hoped the great cloud of dust would hide me
from view.

When I judged we were out of sight of Temperance, I
clambered up the luggage straps and flung myself on top
of the stage. Sometimes there are crates or luggage up
on top but on that hot afternoon there were only a couple
of carpet-bags lashed to the low rail that ran around the
roof. Because the rail was missing at the back, I clung
onto the front part so I would not slide off. Then I made
myself as flat as a postage stamp on a letter.

Once or twice I lifted my head & glanced back to see if
Walt & his pards were in pursuit, but the dust obscured
everything behind me. I tried listening, but it was too
noisy to hear anything apart from the horses' hooves

pounding & their harness jangling & the coach rattling & creaking beneath me.

We had been rocking along for a few minutes when I heard the driver cry 'Whoa!' & I felt the coach slow down.

I was praying, 'No, don't stop.'

I kept my eyes tightly shut until I heard him say. 'Off! You get off now!'

I glanced up. Sure enough, he had twisted round on his seat and was glaring down at me.

He raised his whip & said, 'No Injuns! No danged Heathens allowed. You savvy?'

I lifted up my head & said, 'Please, sir. Please keep driving. My life is in danger. I am not a Heathen. I am a Methodist. Also, I can pay.'

The driver narrowed his eyes. 'You the Reverend's foster kid?' he asked.

'Yes, sir,' I said.

He spat some brown tobacco juice onto the ground. 'I'll let you come along but you have to stay there. Can't have your sort riding down below.'

Ma Evangeline used to say it is a mark of ignorance to despise folk who have different colored skin, because everybody's blood is the same color. I know she is right about this – I have seen enough blood to know – but I always felt different from her and Pa Emmet. Not just from them, but from everybody. I nodded to show the driver I would stay put.

He flicked his whip & the coach rocked forward again.

The dust was settling so I darted a look behind to see if Walt was in pursuit. There was nothing but sage-brush and desert behind us. I was mighty relieved.

I clung on to the rail & pressed myself back down onto the smooth lacquered roof of the coach. It was hot that day & I felt like a fried egg on a griddle as we rattled towards Dayton. I tried closing my eyes, but every time I did that I saw a vision of my ma & pa lying in a pool of blood. So I turned my head to the right & watched the dusty plain pass by.

It wasn't long before the coach slowed a little and I heard the rumble of the wooden bridge as we crossed the Carson River. I lifted my head and saw the flash of a coin flipped by the driver to the toll-house keeper. Then he whipped up the team again, and shortly after we arrived in Dayton.

I go to school in Dayton, but this was the first time I had ever taken the stage to get there.

Dayton used to be called 'Chinatown' because there were so many Chinamen living there. But most of them moved up to Virginia City, or went off to work on the new Rail Road back east. So now it is called Dayton. Pa Emmet told me it is the oldest town in the Territory, though Mormon Station also makes that claim. Both towns came into being in 1849, which makes them 13 years old, a year older than me. But I am older than Virginia City, which has only been around for three or so years.

When the stage stopped outside the Nevada Hotel on

Main St. in Dayton, I lifted my head a little. It was real quiet all of a sudden. I could hear the horses snuffling & snorting, also the voices of men & a woman laughing. The stage rocked a little as someone got on or off. I couldn't be sure & I didn't want to look, in case I betrayed my presence on top.

I could hear a bird singing & I could see the line of cottonwood & willow trees that marked the riverbed. I thought of the school marm, a spinster named Miss Marlowe. She had always been kind to me. I was tempted to get off & ask her to hide me. Maybe I should have.

But I wanted to get as far away from Walt and his gang as I could, so I made the mistake of staying on that stagecoach.

LEDGER SHEET 7

NOT LONG AFTER THE STAGE LEFT DAYTON, WE came to that new toll road that goes up through Gold Canyon. The road curved & twisted between yellow-turning cottonwoods and giant gray rocks. At first the sun was in front of us, for it was late afternoon & we were heading west but soon it travelled along beside us as we headed north. That new road was so smooth that we hardly jounced at all, but the grade was so steep that I had to hang tight to the rail at the front or I would have slid back off the slippery top of the stage.

After maybe half an hour we slowed to a stop. The driver called out, 'Silver City!' & picked up one of the carpet-bags strapped to the rail beside me & tossed it down. Its absence made me feel exposed so I kept my head down while someone got on. Soon we were off again.

Although Virginia City is only a few miles from Dayton, I had never been there before. Ma wanted to look around when we first arrived, but Pa forbade it. He called it Satan's Playground.

He said Virginia City was the vilest place on earth, even worse than San Francisco. He told us that the first 27 men buried in the graveyard had all been murdered. Pa said that you were considered of no account until you 'killed your man'. He said the most respected man in Virginia City was not the preacher or the police chief, but the saloon-keeper with a big diamond pin on his lapel.

Pa once told us there is a whole street for 'Soiled Doves'. When I asked what a Soiled Dove was, he said it was a low-class woman who sparked men for pay. He said you could tell the Soiled Doves by their gaudy dresses trimmed with black lace, and by the fact that they did not wear corsets. I asked him what 'spark' meant. He said it meant to kiss & cuddle. He was going to tell me more but then Ma shushed him.

According to Pa Emmet, Virginia City was also full of Chinamen, Mexicans, Indians, Cornishmen, Irishmen, Miners, Desperados, Gamblers, Gunmen & Lawyers. He said the Lawyers were the worst of all. He called them 'the Devil's Own' & said those smooth-talking crooks could make you give them all you had. He said he would rather dine with a Soiled Dove or a Mississippi Gambler than with one of those Lawyers.

'Devil's Gate!' cried the driver, and I lifted my head to see two demonic rocks rearing up on either side of the road and the stagecoach about to pass between them. As

27

we passed between them, the driver slowed down for a Toll House. I glanced behind me. I could see no riders in pursuit. Should I get off now while the getting was good? Before I could decide, the driver tossed the toll-keeper a coin and lashed the horses & said, 'Heeya!' and we were off again.

There was no going back now.

As we climbed higher & higher up the canyon road, I felt like something was pushing my ears, making them hurt. Then there was a kind of pop in my ears & my head felt empty & I could hear more acutely than ever. That was when I first heard the music of Virginia City.

It was faint at first but soon I could hear it even over the noisy stagecoach: a kind of thumping dirge, deep & low. Mixed up with the rhythmic pounding of horses' hooves and the jingling of the harness it became something like a song. Any noise with a strong slow beat has a peculiar effect on me. It makes me feel calm & floaty, and time seems to dissolve. As the coach went higher, the music of the mountain got louder & I went into a kind of trance. I don't know if it lasted a few minutes or a few hours, but the sudden jolting halt of the stage combined with a shrill mine whistle brought me to my senses.

'Gold Hill,' called the driver. 'Next stop Virginia City!'

I came back to the world like a swimmer surfacing from a deep-flowing river. We had stopped by a hotel near some of the biggest tailings I had seen, like giant anthills streaked with yellow & gold & orange in the hot afternoon sunlight.

I could see some mine buildings further up the sage-dotted slopes & I realized the rhythmic thudding came from the many Quartz Stamp Mills within them. One of these mills stood outside the building rather than inside. It was a door-shaped frame twice as high as the stagecoach with eight metal rods, pumping up & down like the legs of a dancer. Miners shoveled rocks from behind and the pulverized quartz was delivered into the mine building to be turned into silver. Miss Marlowe had explained it once but I did not understand. I reckoned there must be a thousand of them in Virginia City to make the ground throb as if a giant's heart was beating beneath it.

Soon the stage was off again, but slowly this time. Once again the road was climbing steeply & making the poor horses strain. At last we topped a rise & I saw the dome of a barren mountain blotting out half the sky ahead of me. Six or seven streets descended like stairs on that steep mountainside with the top of the stairs on my left and the bottom on my right. Each step was a street of brick or wooden houses with a few tents scattered here & there. We were now following some hay-wagons and our pace had slowed considerably. As we reached the outskirts of the town we ground to halt.

'C Street, Virginia!' cried the driver. 'This coach goes on to the International Hotel but you can get off here if you like. You'll probably be there before us,' I heard him add under his breath.

Below me one of the doors opened & I felt the stage

rock a little & I peeped down to see a pink & black parasol get off. I glanced back one final time to make sure Walt was nowhere around. He wasn't, so I sat up & tapped the driver on the shoulder & when he turned his head I held out my gold coin.

'Shoot,' he said, & spat a stream of tobacco juice at the ground. 'I ain't got change for $20 gold piece. You pay me next time you see me. Get your reverend pa to put in a kind word for me with the Good Lord. Name's Jas Woorstell. Two O's and two L's.'

I nodded & closed my eyes & silently prayed, 'Dear Lord, as my pa is dead and cannot ask you I am asking you myself: please bless Jas Woorstell – two O's and two L's – for his Christian kindness.' Then I eased myself down off the back of the stagecoach & jumped onto the dusty ground.

An empty buckboard had pulled up behind us and there was more traffic behind it.

I thought, 'This C Street appears to be the Main Street.'

Then I thought, 'I'd best get off it, in case Walt and his pards are still in pursuit.'

Feeling breathless and dizzy, I scrambled down a steep road between some sage bushes & shacks & a Mine Building and then I turned left along a dusty but level street & hurried along with my head down for a while.

By and by I thought, 'I have arrived in Satan's Playground. I had better get my bearings.'

So I stopped and looked around.

Dayton has two Chinese laundries, but this appeared to be a whole street of them, along with a lumberyard & a brewery & some more tailings. Steam & smoke rose from the roofs of wooden shacks crammed side by side. I could smell lye and starch. Lines of clothing flapped in the late afternoon breeze & some sheets were even laid out on the roofs of the shacks. There were Chinese people everywhere. A few signs were in Chinese letters but most were in English. They said things like SEE YUP, WASHER & IRONER and SAM SING & AH HOP, WASHING.

There was a water pump outside one of the laundries right there at the side of the street. I was mighty dusty from riding on top of the stage, so I went over to it & pumped some water & splashed it on my face. Then I pumped some more and bent my head to drink when a woman's voice called out 'Stop! Don't drink that! It's poison!'

LEDGER SHEET 8

'**Stop!**' cried a woman. '**No drinkee!**'

I turned & saw that it was the woman with the parasol from the stage. She had brown hair with a little feathered hat perched on top and a puffy red and pink dress.

She said, 'No drinkee water. It heap bad medicine.'

I said, 'Beg pardon?'

She said, 'Oh! You speak English. I thought you were an Injun. I wanted to warn you that the water hereabouts is undrinkable. It is tainted with arsenic, plumbago and copperas.'

I did not know what any of those things were but they sounded nasty.

I said, 'What do people drink?'

She said, 'Mainly whiskey.' She smiled. I could not tell if it was Smile No. 1 or Smile No. 2.

I studied her carefully. Her red and pink dress was

puffy below the waist & skimpy above. It had some faded black lace on it & I judged it had seen better days. Her fringed parasol matched the dress. She also had a pearly fan and a pretty beaded purse.

She tipped her head on one side and said, 'Wasn't it nice of the driver to let you keep your $20 gold piece?'

I said, 'Are you a Soiled Dove?'

The woman's eyes opened wide. They were as blue as the sky above.

I said, 'The reason I asked if you are a Soiled Dove is this: my dead pa used to say that women who wear red and black lace are usually Soiled Doves, but I see you are wearing a corset, so I cannot be sure.'

'Well, yes,' she said, fanning herself. 'I suppose you could call me a Soiled Dove, only it is not real polite to call a person that to her face. I prefer the term "Actress".'

'I'm sorry, ma'am,' I said. 'I did not mean to offend you.'

'Then no offense taken.' She looked me up and down. 'Can you tell me why you are dressed like an Injun but speak like an American?'

'I am half white, ma'am. My name is P.K. Pinkerton.'

'Pleased to meet you, P.K. My name is Belle Donne.'

She held out her hand. She was wearing dusty black gloves. I shook it. She smelled of rose oil and whiskey.

'I was just visiting a gentleman friend over in Como,' she said, 'but I live here in Virginia, in a crib up on D Street.'

'How can you live in a crib?' I said. 'That is where babies sleep.'

She said, 'Here in Virginia they call a one-room frame-house a crib. It must be your first time up here.'

'Yes, ma'am. We only moved to Dayton four months ago.'

She was still smiling. 'Would you like me to show you around?'

I nodded. I was glad to have a resident of the place show me around, even if she was a low-class woman who sometimes sparked men for pay.

Belle gestured at the dusty street with her fan. 'This is F Street. People here call it Chinatown. Many people despise the Celestials and only tolerate them because they are the best launderers. However, I like them. I find them to be even-tempered & calm. I live up on D Street but I intend to move up to A Street as soon as I can bag a rich banker or broker. See up there?' She used her folded fan to point up the mountain. 'The most desirable houses are highest up. They have hardly any shootings.'

I said, 'Shootings?'

She said, 'You often see men shooting at each other right out in the open. But they don't mean nothing by it. It's just that people drink a lot of liquor here in Virginia and everybody carries a gun.'

'Do you carry a gun?' I said.

'Of course.' She fished down the front of her low-cut dress & pulled out a small Deringer handgun with an engraved barrel and walnut grip.

I swallowed hard. My pa had warned me about Virginia City. I had not been here two minutes & had already met a pistol-packing Soiled Dove & heard of drunken murder in the streets.

She said, 'This piece may look small, but it has a few surprises.' She replaced the Deringer & said, 'Carson mills silver under trees some where.'

I said, 'Beg pardon?'

We were walking north now, with the mountain on our left. Belle Donne said, 'When I first moved here three months ago, I devised a clever way to learn the names of the streets. All the streets named after letters run north to south and they are flat as pancakes. It is the crossroads that give you trouble. They are real steep and their names are not as easy to remember as ABC. So I made up a sentence using the first letters of each: Carson Mills Silver Under Trees Some Where. That stands for Carson Street, Mill Street, Sutton, Union, Taylor, Smith and Washington.'

I said, 'Carson Mills Silver Under Trees Some Where. That is clever. What is that street up ahead?'

Belle said, 'That is Mill Street. We will turn up it & then double back to my place on D Street. My crib is not far as the crow flies but, as you see, Chinatown and the steepness of the cliff and the lumberyard along with the tailings of the mines and so forth means there are no cross streets here.'

She was right. I could see the next street up above us, but no easy way of getting there.

'What are you doing here in Virginia, P.K.?' said Belle Donne as we walked along.

I felt dizzy so I took a breath & said, 'Some desperados disguised as Indians just murdered my foster parents. They are after me. I only escaped because I am dressed like an Indian, too. I do not think they were expecting that.'

'Oh.' She pressed her fingers to the base of her throat & stopped walking. 'Why did they kill your foster parents? And why are they after you?'

We had stopped outside a laundry. The sign had some Chinese writing & below it: HONG WO, WASHER. There was a boy about my age or a little older standing in the front yard. He had his back to us & he was pegging up sheets. He wore a faded blue collarless shirt & loose blue trowsers & a dusty black skullcap. He had a long black pigtail.

Belle looked at me & I looked at her.

I said, 'I am not sure if I can trust you. The stagecoach let us off on C Street and you live on D Street so why are you down here on F Street? I reckon you followed me.'

Belle laughed. 'The reason I came down here was to pick up some washing from Mr. Yup, but it was not quite ready. Then I saw you about to taste that poisonous water and thought it was my Christian duty to help.' She smiled and fanned herself. 'So tell me why those men are after you.'

Her smile was so pretty that I reckoned it was Expression No. 1: a Genuine Smile.

'I think they want this,' I said. I pulled out my medicine bag & took out the Letter & handed it to her.

She took it & opened it but frowned when she saw it. 'Do I look like a school marm?'

I thought of Miss Marlowe in Dayton who always wears dark colors with long sleeves and a buttoned up neck. 'No, ma'am,' I said. 'You do not look like a school marm.'

She sighed deeply and rolled her eyes. 'I cannot read fancy writing like that. Please read it to me.'

I read it to her.

'Why, P.K.,' said Belle Donne when I finished. 'I believe that Letter is a kind of Last Will & Testament. I have never heard of Pleasant Town or Sun Peak but it might refer to land hereabouts, because it names the Divide.'

'What is the Divide?' I asked.

Belle pointed with her fan. 'It is that there hump in the mountainside we just came over, that had our horses straining so. It lies between Virginia and Gold Hill.'

I said, 'Do you think I could get money for this Letter?' I noticed that the Chinese boy had stopped pegging up sheets & was watching us.

'I am sure of it,' she said. Her eyes were real bright. 'If desperados want it badly enough to kill for it, why then it is probably worth a thousand dollars at least. You should take it to the Recorder's Office and show it to them. Or perhaps a Lawyer.'

I said, 'Lawyers are the Devil's Own. I will not have anything to do with them.' I folded up the Letter & put it back in my medicine bag. 'Where is the Recorder's Office?'

'There is one up on A Street near Sutton across from the Newspaper. I believe there is also one in Gold Hill, on the other side of the Divide.'

I said, 'A Street near Sutton.' Then I repeated, 'Carson Mills Silver Under Trees Some Where.'

Belle Donne was looking back along F Street, the way we had come. Her eyes were wide & she was pressing her fingers to the base of her throat again.

'P.K.,' she said. 'How many desperados dressed as Injuns are after you and that Letter?'

'Three,' I said.

'Riding two horses and a mule?'

'Yes, ma'am.'

'Get behind me, P.K. They are coming this way.'

LEDGER SHEET 9

WALT & HIS TWO PARDS WERE RIDING SLOWLY DOWN F Street, looking left and right.

They did not look excited nor had they spurred their mounts to a gallop, so I judged they had not seen me. But any moment they would. I desperately looked around for a place to hide.

'P.K.,' said Belle Donne. 'Climb under my skirt.'

It was a strange request but I saw immediately that she was right. Unless one of the Celestials would instantly give me shelter, the only place to hide was under her big, hoop skirt. Quick as a telegram, I darted underneath it.

It was like being in a pink tent with two slender legs instead of a tent pole. Belle Donne was wearing ruffled white bloomers & white stockings & dusty black ankle boots with about a dozen hooked buttons on each side. It was cool under there, but also dusty. I felt my nose prickle.

I scrouched down under there and waited. My mouth

was dry. I could feel the mountain thumping & I could hear a donkey braying & some Celestials arguing in Chinese. I heard some quail in the sage. They were crying, 'Chicago! Chi-ca-go!' the way they do. Then I heard the clop of horses getting nearer. Then the clopping stopped & I heard the jingle of a bridle & Walt's voice saying. 'Excuse me, ma'am, but did you just get off the stage from Como?'

'Yes, sir, I did.'

The dust under Belle Donne's hoop skirt was making my nose prickle real bad. I stifled a sneeze by pinching my nostrils shut.

'Do you remember,' said Walt, 'was there a boy on board? About twelve years old? Only he run away from Temperance and his relatives have sent us to fetch him back.'

'I'm sorry,' said Miss Donne. 'But I do not recall seeing a boy on board.'

I did not know it then, but the air in Virginia is real thin & when you first arrive you can feel sick & dizzy. I was feeling its effects just then & the ground started to tip to one side. To steady myself, I let go of my nose and grabbed hold of Belle Donne's knees.

'Oooh!' said Belle Donne.

'Are you all right, ma'am?' said Walt's voice.

'Yes,' said Belle Donne. 'Yes, I believe it is only a flea in my corset. It made me jump.'

'I would be happy to fetch it out for you,' said Raspy Voice.

I was still clinging to Belle's legs & I felt them trembling.

'Not now, Dub,' said Walt. 'We got other fish to fry.'

I heard the creak of a saddle & the soft slurring sound of horses' hooves in the dust as they turned to go.

Then I did the worst possible thing: I sneezed violently.

There was a pause & then a flood of light & Belle's voice saying, 'Run for it, P.K.! Run!'

My eyes were dazzled by the sunlight after the pink gloom of Belle's skirt, and I only caught a quick glimpse of three men looking down at us from their mounts. I could not see their features, just that they were wearing hats and long duster coats. Then I felt Belle grasp my hand and pull me past the open-mouthed Chinese boy towards an alley between two wash houses.

I do not like people to touch me but this time I did not protest. I followed her through hanging sheets that wetly slapped our faces. I let go her hand as we plunged into the alley. The walls of the huts on either side were so close to each other that they shmooshed her skirt and I had to follow three feet behind. Belle led me this way and that, through a maze of alleys & between more wet sheets with the smell of lye very strong & the Celestials staring at us as we passed.

'Here,' she said breathlessly. 'In here!'

She pulled me into a wash house full of big wooden vats of sudsy water & more staring Celestials & back out into an alley. She looked around frantically, then pulled me through a door with only a curtain across it. We found ourselves in a hot and steamy shack that smelled of starch. There were maybe five Chinese men standing behind tables with flat irons sending up clouds of steam. They looked up at us with puffy chipmunk cheeks as we came in, then went back to their ironing as if there was nothing strange about a Soiled Dove and an Indian Youth barging into their workhouse. There were two small wooden tables in the center of the room. These were piled high with clean sheets waiting to be ironed. Some of the sheets were falling down around the table legs. Belle ran to one of the tables and tugged the sheets further down to make a kind of tent.

When I went to join her she pushed me away.

'You go under that one,' she said. 'There ain't room for both of us under mine.' So I went under the other table and pulled some of my sheets down to hide me from view. When I was satisfied that nobody coming in would suspect my hiding place, I parted two of my hanging sheets and peeped out. The door we had come through was only covered by a cloth curtain which occasionally swelled to let out steam from the room and then subsided again.

Watching the Celestials at work, I understood why they had bulging cheeks. It was because their mouths were full of water. They would expertly squirt this water from their mouths onto the sheets & then slam down their flat irons to make hissing clouds of starchy steam billow up.

Over at Belle's table, I could see her pink hoop skirt

sticking out from under the sheets she had draped to hide her from sight. But whenever she pulled it in on one side it would pop out the other. When I heard the menacing jingle of spurred boots coming closer & closer, I began to worry.

My heart nearly stopped when the cloth over the door was wrenched aside & the steam parted to show a man in a black slouch hat and biscuit-colored duster.

I knew it was Walt or one of his men.

He glared around and just at that moment some of Belle's hoop skirt popped out from under the sheets.

'There you are!' cried Whiny Voice & his spurs jangled as he strode towards her with purpose and intent.

LEDGER SHEET 10

As the whiny voiced desperado in the black hat stomped towards Belle's hiding place, I took action. I slipped out from under my table & grabbed a cold flat iron from an empty table & I threw it at him.

Whiny yelled & staggered back & clutched his face with his free hand. His nose was spurting blood.

When the Celestials saw their shed full of snowy white sheets endangered by this flood of crimson, they sprang into action. Three of them shoved Whiny back out of the starching shed. Another one grabbed me, and the last one yanked Belle from her hiding place. In a moment they had ejected all three of us into the alley outside. They were shouting at us in Chinese.

'Dang you!' cried Whiny, shaking himself free of the Celestials and rounding on me. 'You broke my nose! I'm gonna kill you both!' He pulled out a Colt's Navy Revolver from the right hand pocket of his duster coat & cocked it & drew a bead on me.

But before he could pull the trigger, a shot rang out. Belle had fired her Pocket Pistol. The ball must have struck the desperado in his hand or wrist because his gun flew up in the air and fell down. As it struck the ground it went off with a bang & the man yelped. 'I been shot!' Whiny held up one foot and we saw the heel of his boot had been shot off. 'Shot by my own piece!' He held up his bloody hand. 'And you creased my thumb, you blank!'

'You make one move,' said Belle, lowering the gaze of her Pistol, 'and I will shoot you in your Privates. Now get your hands up!'

'You already shot your load,' he said with a sneer.

'This here's a Double Deringer,' said Belle. 'You can see that it has only one barrel but two hammers. There is another .41 caliber ball in there just waiting to be discharged.'

'You filthy Hurdy!' he said. But he held up his hands. Blood was still leaking from his flattened nose & he looked at us with a kind of squint. I knew from his whiny voice that he was the one ma Evangeline had brained with the skillet.

Belle quickly used her left hand to pat him down. She found a few silver dollars and some paper money. She stuffed these down the front of her neckline and then said, 'Close your eyes, you ugly Varmint, and count to a hundred!'

Whiny did as he was ordered. While his eyes were squinched shut and his lips were mouthing the numbers,

Belle grabbed my hand & pulled me through the crowd of Celestials. They had stopped yelling and were watching us with interest.

I dropped Belle's hand soon after and followed her through a corral with a few horses in it. She slipped in some manure and cursed, using language unfit for publication. I helped her up and soon we were out of the corral & clambering up a steep slope between a lumberyard and the back of a brewery.

We made it up to the next street and Belle picked up her soiled skirts and ran. Her hair was coming unpinned & her feathered hat bobbed up and down like a dead bird on its perch.

We were on a flat street now. I followed her past lots of little wooden shacks & a few brick houses & a tent or two. Some of the shacks had blue or red lamps in the windows. There were a fair number of houses under construction & even a few lots vacant.

Chinatown had been a warren of narrow alleys, but this street was wide enough for traffic. I saw carriages & mule carts & a milk wagon. The big horses pulling the milk wagon shied as Belle Donne swished past and their driver had to calm them.

A shiny black buggy approached and as it passed the lady driver called out. 'Are you in a hurry, Belle? Do you need a ride?' She was a pretty woman in a frothy lemon-colored dress & matching bonnet. She did not wait for a reply but laughed and touched her white horses with a whip.

I heard Belle mutter something about 'Danged Short Sally and her airs,' and then she had crossed the street and was squishing her skirt so she could pass through the open doorway of a half-built frame-house. The structure had walls, but no doors or glass in yet, and no roof. We sat with our backs against the wall beneath an empty window. Being unused to such thin air, I was gasping for breath. I felt dizzy and for a moment I thought I might pass out.

As I began to recover, I glanced around. This must be one of the cribs Belle had mentioned. The shadow of the mountain had started to creep over the town and I guessed the workmen had gone home. Either that or they had run out of funds and temporarily abandoned it. Because it had no roof, I was able to look up & see a few clouds in the deep blue sky above. They were lit pink & gold from the setting sun.

Outside on the road, I heard the comforting sound of normal traffic. My sharp ears detected no jangly spurs or urgent hoofbeats in pursuit.

Belle was fiddling with her hat, trying to pin it back into place. 'I would love a smart little rig like Sally's,' she said, her chest still rising & falling. 'And two ponies of my own. I could keep them up at the Flora Temple Livery Stable.' She patted her hat, which was only a little crooked.

I held onto the sill of the unglazed window & lifted my head & peeped out.

'I think the coast is clear,' I said, and glanced over at

Belle. She had emptied the contents of her purse onto the raw plank floor. I saw a small powder flask & a rammer & some little brass percussion caps. She was reloading the strange gun with its single barrel and two hammers. I saw it took grooved balls the size of chickpeas. She must have noticed my interest for she said, 'This here is a Double Deringer. A Mr. Lindsay invented it after his brother was attacked by two Injuns and he only had one ball in his pistol.'

'May I see it?'

'I'm afraid not,' said Belle, pressing the second percussion cap on.

She raised the freshly loaded Deringer and pointed it at my heart. 'I am going to have to ask you to give me your $20 gold coin,' she said. 'And that Thousand Dollar Letter, too.'

LEDGER SHEET 11

I STARED AT BELLE DONNE IN DISMAY.

Her blue eyes glittered and her cheeks were real pink.

'You will soon learn,' she said. 'It is every man for himself here in Virginia. And every woman, too. Now give me what you have there.'

This is what I was thinking: 'Once again my Thorn has led me into trouble.'

I quickly glanced around, looking for something to fight back with. But there was not a single spare plank of wood and I still felt dizzy.

She cocked both hammers of her strange handgun. 'Do not even think about it,' she said. 'Give me what I asked for.'

I reached into my medicine pouch and took out the $20 coin and the folded up Letter and handed them over. Without taking her eyes from me she opened her beaded wrist bag and put those two things inside.

She gestured with her Double Deringer. 'What else have you got in there?'

'Nothing,' I said. 'Just my Indian ma's flint knife and my pa's Detective Button.'

She said, 'What is a Detective Button?'

I did not reply.

'Tell me,' she said. 'Or I will shoot you.'

I took the button out of my right hand pocket and showed it to her. 'It is a button from my dead pa's jacket,' I said. 'It is all I have of his. He was a Rail Road Detective.'

She frowned. 'What is a Detective?'

'A Detective is a person who uncovers crimes by following clews. Like Mr. Bucket in Bleak House. A Rail Road Detective protects people and goods on the train.'

She said, 'Who is Mr. Bucket and what is a Bleak House?'

'He is an invented character in a book by Charles Dickens,' I said. 'Have you never heard of Dickens?'

She did not answer my question. Instead she said, 'Is that button valuable?'

'Only to me,' I said. 'It has sentimental value.'

'You do not seem to be a sentimental type of person to me,' said Belle Donne. 'You are a cold and heartless child to be able to speak of your parents' death with no emotion.'

'That is my Thorn,' I said. 'I cannot express emotions easily. Nor read them neither. But I will miss my ma and pa dearly.'

She said, 'Did they ever beat you?'

'No.'

'Then you should count yourself lucky.'

I said, 'I do count myself lucky. They were both real good to me. Ma Evangeline taught me to read and write and Pa Emmet taught me the Word of God.'

Belle Donne said, 'Turn around and sit Injun fashion. I am going to bind your hands.'

I turned around and sat cross-legged.

I felt her bind up my wrists behind me. Later I found out she used a red ribbon from her hat.

I said, 'What you are doing is wrong.'

She said, 'I need that gold coin more than you do, P.K. I have a bad habit.'

I said, 'All I want is enough money to get me a ticket to Chicago.'

'Lie down on your side,' said Belle, 'and bend your knees. I am going to tie your ankles to your wrists.' As she bound my ankles she said, 'What is in Chicago?'

'My uncle Allan Pinkerton runs a National Detective Agency out of Chicago. He has lots of Detectives working for him, including some women.'

'Does he?' She pulled my feet back towards my hands.

'Yes. One of them is named Miss Kate Warne. She disguises herself and pretends to be someone she's not.' I quoted from a newspaper Ma Evangeline had once showed me. *'In this clever guise Miss Kate Warne obtains confessions from the culprits.* Sometimes she "shadows" people,' I added. 'That means she follows them.'

51

'How do you know that?' said Belle as she tied my ankles together.

'It was in a newspaper.' I turned my head and tried to look over my shoulder at her. 'I reckon if my uncle employs women as Detectives, then he might hire children, too. Especially if they are his own flesh and blood. If I could get to Chicago, I feel sure my uncle could use me in his Detective Agency as a Private Eye.' I added, 'If I can overcome my Thorn.'

'What is a "Private Eye"?' she asked, as she bound my ankles to my wrists.

I said, 'A Private Eye is a person you hire to spy out the Truth for you.'

'Well, I hope you succeed,' she said as she tied off the ribbon. 'But right now I need that coin and I need that Letter.'

I said, 'I saved your life back there when I hit Walt's pard.'

She gasped. '*Whose* pard?'

'Walt's. That's what they were calling him, anyways.'

Her face came into view as she moved around in front of me. 'That man was Whittlin Walt?' she said. The color had gone right out of her face and her voice was breathy.

'Not the one you shot,' I said. 'The other one. The one who spoke to you when I was hiding under your skirt.'

'He was Whittlin Walt?'

'I do not know his full name,' I said. 'I only know the other two called him Walt.'

'Dear God.' She buried her face in her black-gloved hands. 'Oh dear God, no!'

'What's wrong?' I said.

'Whittlin Walt is the most feared outlaw in the Territory,' she said. Her voice was muffled by her hands. 'Do you know why they call him Whittlin Walt?'

'No.'

She lifted her face and looked at me with one of the few expressions I can easily recognize: Fear.

She said, 'They call him Whittlin Walt because he whittles pieces off his victims while they are still alive.'

LEDGER SHEET 12

BELLE WAS OUT THE DOOR AND RUNNING BEFORE I could ask her to tell me more about this terrible desperado who was after me.

My first acquaintance in Virginia City had robbed me and tied me up. My wrists and feet were bound and I was lying on my left side on planks of raw wood. I considered myself lucky she had not gagged me, too. Dusk was here and soon it would be night.

It seemed to me there was only one thing I could do. Yell for help.

However, I do not like having to yell for help.

I do not even like having to ask for help.

I like to do things myself.

It was getting darker by the moment.

I heard some quail in the sage somewhere nearby. They said, 'Chicago! Chicago!' as if to remind me of my goal.

Then I heard a chorus of coyote yips down in the

canyon. Coyotes will eat just about anything and I knew they would not turn up their noses at me because I was half Sioux and half White. That decided me: I did not want to be eaten alive by coyotes.

'Help!' I cried. 'Help me please! I have been robbed and I am lying tied up in this half-finished crib. I do not want to be eaten alive by coyotes!'

I had only been yelling a short time when I heard a footfall outside the open doorway and I caught my breath. I suddenly realized that the only people who cared to find me were Whittlin Walt and his two pards.

Had my shouts brought them right to me?

At that moment, fighting off a passel of hungry coyotes seemed preferable to facing Whittlin Walt and his Bowie Knife.

I closed my eyes and tried The Half-Finished House Trick. That is where you pretend to be a half-finished House and hope you blend in.

It did not work.

My nose caught the scent of lye and of something chemical but unfamiliar. I opened my eyes to see two wooden soled sandals. Above the sandals were a pair of loose, faded blue pantaloons, and above that a blue shirt and a Chinese boy looking down at me. I could not read his expression.

He squatted down. 'Be quiet, Fool!' he hissed. 'I think the man who is after you is nearby!' He began to fumble with the knotted ribbon around my wrists. He was trying to untie me.

I said, 'In the medicine bag around my neck there is a flint knife.'

He found my medicine bag and took out the stone blade. With a few swift strokes he cut me free.

'Come!' he said, handing back the flint and the bits of red ribbon Belle had used. 'Chop, chop!' He pulled me roughly out through an opening in the wall for a back door.

My wrists hurt and my ankles had pins and needles but I managed to stumble after him up a dusty slope. Both of us used stunted sage bushes as hand-holds to pull ourselves up. We startled the family of quail who had been urging me to go to Chicago. They skedaddled.

The slope here was so steep that some of the buildings had their nether regions propped up on tall stilts. The young Celestial took me under one of these, where the shadows were deepest. He stopped and looked quickly around to make sure the coast was clear. Then we scrambled up more slope until we reached a kind of alley between two wooden buildings. I am not plump, or even stocky, but I could barely squeeze through. The Chinese boy was taller than me but maybe a little skinnier. I reckoned he had not been dining as well as I had.

At last we emerged from the alley onto a dusty street with crowded boardwalks either side. I had never seen so many people crammed together in one place. In the jostling crowd I could hear women laughing & men shouting & music playing. The noise was made louder because lots of buildings had balconies which formed a kind of roof over the walkways & threw back the noise. Some of the buildings were wood, some were brick & over on the corner to our right was a six-sided mansion made of gray stone. The street was full of carts and carriages, all sending up clouds of dust.

'Skirt boy!' said the Celestial. 'Stop staring. Follow me.'

'Skirt boy?' I said.

'I saw you hiding under skirt of bad woman. I follow you.'

Then I knew he was the boy who had been pegging up sheets outside HONG WO, WASHER.

I said, 'You are the boy who was pegging up sheets outside Hong Wo, Washer. My name is P.K. Pinkerton. Thank you for rescuing me.'

He said, 'I am Ping. Now shut up and come. Chop, chop! I am taking you to a place where you can change clothes. You stand out like a cricket in a bowl of rice.'

I had no choice but to follow him & hope he would not try to rob & kill me as Belle had done. As he led me through the jostling crowds along the creaking boardwalk, I observed that almost all the men were miners. I could tell because they sported flannel shirts & pantaloons & knee-high boots & bushy beards. The men outnumbered the women about ten to one.

I noticed that every other building we passed appeared to be a saloon or a hurdy-hall. I could tell because I could hear music coming out: 'Camptown Races' mostly. But there were other buildings apart from saloons. I saw a Dry Goods Store, an Assay Office, a Wells Fargo Bank, etc. There was even a Chinese Laundry up here.

People were looking at me and suddenly a woman with yellow ringlets and a low cut pink bodice caught my arm and turned me to face her.

'Oh, look,' she said. 'A sweet little Injun boy all in fringed deerskin. Ain't he pretty?'

The man beside her spat tobacco juice onto the boardwalk near my feet.

Ping was right: I stuck out like a cricket in a bowl of rice.

Beckoning me to follow, Ping jumped down off the boardwalk onto the wide & dusty street. He crossed in the gap between two slow moving lumber wagons.

As I stepped out from the awning to follow him I saw a big brick building across the way. It was the fanciest building I had ever seen. It was three stories tall, with shops on the street level & columns holding up a balcony that ran all around the front & side with big arched windows leading out onto it. A lofty sign near the top of the building announced that this was the INTERNATIONAL HOTEL. Another sign on the part that curved around the corner read: OFFICE CAL. STAGE Co. I thought, 'That must be where the stagecoach to Chicago stops.'

The crack of a whip and a juicy oath brought me to my senses and I got out of the way of a brace of oxen just in time not to be trampled to a paste. Looking both ways, I hurried across the dusty street after Ping. He was up on the boardwalk talking to a Chinaman who was dressed in a suit like a banker. I jumped up, too, and waited.

Ping and his friend seemed to be embroiled in some deep argument, so I wandered over to look at a notice outside the International Hotel. You show me something once and I never forget it. This is what the sign said,

New INTERNATIONAL HOTEL

PROPRIETORS

A.S. PAUL & I. BATEMAN

ARE PLEASED TO ANNOUNCE THE OPENING OF THE

FINEST HOTEL
OF THE TERRITORY

Featuring

a Parlor 18 by 20 feet, & also 10 bed-rooms, so arranged that two of them can be thrown together, so as to make bed-room & parlor for families. From the roof of the house, which is surrounded by a fire wall three feet high, a magnificent view of Virginia City & the surrounding country can be obtained. A flag-staff, 40 feet in height, is also placed there. The building is entirely fire-proof. The iron work upon the house alone cost over $4,000. The entire cost of this new building, exclusive of furniture, was $14,000. (The old building on B Street will still be continued as a portion of the Hotel, & will shortly be superseded by a continuation of the new one.)

STAGES leave the **INTERNATIONAL HOTEL** every Day
connecting with all prominent places in
California & Nevada Territory.
The **BAR** is supplied with the choicest

WINES, LIQUORS AND CIGARS

And every modern improvement is continually added, making this
THE HOTEL OF THE TERRITORY

After I read that sign I went to look in the window of Wasserman's Emporium and to admire the painted plaster statue of a man outside a Shooting Gallery.

Ping was still arguing, so I sidled down to where the Stagecoach Office was situated, keeping an eye out for Walt & his men and also for Belle.

When I got to the corner, a crudely painted street sign told me that I was on C street & Union. C Street was flat, but Union was the steepest side street I had seen yet. It was so steep that it made the International Hotel look like a wedge of cake on its side, with the frosting its front & the tapering part its back.

Then I found what I was looking for. On the outside wall of the Office of the Cal Stage Company was a list of stagecoach destinations & prices. I ran my finger down until I found the fare from Virginia City to Chicago.

It was $100.

That seemed a Vast Fortune.

I needed to find Belle and get my Letter back. Then I could buy a ticket to Chicago and get out of this place where every man and beast seemed so intent on killing me.

I was just turning back to see if Ping was coming when I heard the crack of a pistol, and a man came running along the boardwalk straight towards me.

LEDGER SHEET 13

THERE WAS A BIG WOODEN BARREL OUTSIDE THE Office of the Cal Stage Company. I dived behind it as the gunman came running towards me. He was a beardless blond and he was firing an old Colt's Dragoon Revolver into the air. It made a thunderous noise and produced a fair amount of smoke. He fired four more shots and kept pulling the trigger even after the chambers were empty and the gun went click. Then he fell down onto the boardwalk almost at my feet. A woman screamed & a horse tied to a hitching post reared up, but most people laughed.

I did not think he was Walt or one of his men but I gave a sniff just in case. I could not detect the smell of Bay Rum Hair Tonic. But I could smell whiskey.

People had come up and were bending over him.

'Is he dead?' I heard one bearded miner ask.

'Nah, he's just drunk,' said another. He held up the big Colt's Dragoon. 'And I got me a new gun. Yee haw!'

The man put the unloaded revolver in his waistband &
then ran off down the boardwalk whooping.

I felt a hand grip my arm so hard that it hurt. It was
Ping.

'Chop, chop!' he said. 'I must get you to a safe place.'

I let him pull me away from the drunken gunman
and around the corner. We went up the steep side street
called Union, then turned left onto one of the flat letter
streets. I guessed it was B Street as we had been going
up the mountain.

Even though we were keeping to the outside of the
boardwalk, people kept jostling us. I suppose a Chinese
boy and an Indian did not command much respect here.
At one point we had to squeeze through a group of men
in frock coats & plug hats. They were fat & smoking big
cigars & behaving as if they owned the place. I reckon
they were Lawyers. We passed two more Saloons, a
Restaurant and a Saddle Maker's.

Up ahead, I saw another cross street and I said to
myself, 'Carson Mills Silver Under Trees Some Where.
Trees equals Taylor.'

Sure enough, another crudely painted notice on a side
of a building told me it was Taylor Street.

We let a four-mule cart rattle by and then we crossed
over.

'Where are you taking me?' I asked Ping.

'I bring you here.'

He had stopped in front of a shop on the east side of
B Street. Ping tried the door handle. It was locked. He

took a key from his pocket and as he unlocked the door I took a step back to see what shop would offer me shelter. A neatly painted sign read: Isaiah Coffin's Ambrotype & Photographic Gallery.

At that moment, I caught the familiar scent of Pa Emmet's pipe and turned to see a girl about my age emerging from the shop next door. The sign above that door read: Bloomfield's Tobacco Emporium.

The girl had curly brown hair and big brown eyes. As she looked at me her eyes seemed to grow even larger. Was it Expression No. 4: Surprise? Or something else? Yet again, I wished I knew how to read people. I wondered if she wanted to kill me, too.

Before the curly-haired girl could pull out a six-shooter and fill me full of lead, Ping had opened the door of the Photographic Gallery & yanked me roughly inside.

A bell tinkled as the door closed behind us.

It was dim in Isaiah Coffin's Ambrotype & Photographic Gallery & the room smelled of strange chemicals. There was a wooden counter on the left and a big picture window straight ahead and on the right a painted canvas backdrop showing a herd of Buffalo & a Wagon Train on the Great Plains. The artist had put Indian Tee-Pees in the background and also some clouds and mountains. It brought back sad memories.

In front of the painted backdrop were two chairs with dangling fringe on their arms and between them a couch with a buffalo skin draped over it. There was also something that looked like a black accordion with wood and brass at either end. It was fixed to a sturdy walnut frame with cast iron feet.

'This is studio of Isaiah Coffin,' said Ping. 'He is best photographer west of Rockies. I work for him sometimes. He not here right now. You wait. Sleep in buffalo skin in there.' He pointed to a door half hidden by the canvas backdrop. 'Lots of costumes in there,' he said. 'He stores them for a theater friend. Sometimes customers dress up for picture. Costs more.'

I pointed at the black and wood accordion. 'Is that a camera?' I said.

Ping ignored my question. 'You change clothes! I have to go now but tomorrow early I will take you to Territorial Enterprise Newspaper. My uncle Joe works there. His boss will help you find that Lady and Thousand Dollar Letter.'

'How do you know about my Thousand Dollar Letter?' I said.

'I hear you talking to that lady,' said Ping.

'Why are you doing this?' I asked.

He folded his arms across his chest. 'I do this for money,' he said. 'I want half. Five hundred dollar. Agreed?'

I was beginning to understand Virginia City. Nobody ever did anything through Christian kindness. The sooner I got out of here the better.

'Agreed?' said Ping. He wore a scowl and even I could tell he was angry.

I said, 'I was led to believe that all Celestials were even-tempered & calm.'

His scowl deepened. 'Agreed?' he said. 'Five hundred dollar?'

I said, 'All right. But only if I can get cash money for that Letter. Agreed?'

'Agreed.'

He stuck out his hand and I shook it even though I do not like touching people.

He said, 'You stay here. I see you early morning. No touch anything. No let him find you here or he get angry.' Ping gave me the key. 'Lock door after I go.'

'Ain't you staying?' I asked him.

He said, 'Uncle mad at me. Other uncle. Hong Wo, not Old Joe. I must go now or he will beat me.'

The bell tinkled & the door slammed & my scowling rescuer was gone.

I stared at the door. I was scared & tired & hungry. My foster parents were dead & scalped because of me. I had nothing but a flint knife and a Detective Button and a set of clothes that made me look like a cricket in a rice bowl. Added to that, I had three murderous desperados on my tail.

I thought, 'Can anything else go wrong?'

(As I am now writing this at the bottom of a 200 ft mine with those three desperados still on my scent, you will judge that plenty else went wrong.)

LEDGER SHEET 14

AFTER PING CLOSED THE DOOR BEHIND HIM, I locked it as ordered.

Then I went through the open door into the costume cupboard. It smelled of wool & mothballs & lavender & it was filled with more clothing than I had ever seen in one place.

I saw costumes with velvet and ruffs like in a Shakespeare play Ma Evangeline took me to one time. But there were also modern clothes like a miner's getup of knee-high black boots, canvas pantaloons, a red flannel shirt, etc. Also a Banker's Suit and a Fireman's Uniform and some Ladies' clothes including corsets & hoops for under their skirts.

I guessed Isaiah Coffin's Theater Friend liked to put on modern shows as well as old fashioned ones.

There was even half a rack of Mexican, Chinese & Indian outfits. The Indian clothes were fancy: with more fringe &

beads than my buckskins, & even a feathered headdress.

There was the dark blue overcoat of a Union officer & pants to match. Hooked over the hanger was a Colt's Baby Dragoon Revolver like my Indian ma used to carry, only this one had an ivory grip. I thought such a weapon might prove useful. I checked it was unloaded & tested it, but the hammer was busted and it would not fire. I put it back on the hanger.

I thought, 'I would like to see a play with all these characters in it.'

Then, behind one of the big racks I found the best thing of all: it was a smaller rack of children's clothes.

As I looked through the garments, one item gave me an idea. It was a long-sleeved dress made of red calico with little white flowers on it, so when you looked at it from a distance it seemed pink. It had white lace frills around the collar & the cuffs. Also on the hanger was a matching bonnet & there were white socks & bloomers, and little white boots like Belle Donne's. There were two small women's wigs, as well. One with curly blonde ringlets. One with dark ringlets.

I reached up & stroked my head. I have straight black hair. It is short because last month I had nits & Ma Evangeline washed my hair in turpentine & when that did not vanquish the vermin she shaved my head.

I pulled the blonde wig over my head and inspected myself in a tall & narrow mirror on the wall. The golden curls looked wrong with my sallow complexion & dark eyes. But the dark wig with its dangling ringlets transformed me.

I took off my buckskins and put on stockings & bloomers & a chemise & a white petticoat & over it the calico dress.

The lace trim prickled my skin. Next I put on the white ankle boots. They just about fit. It took me a long time to do up all the little buttons with a button-hook. The wig and bonnet formed the finishing touch. Dressing as a girl was time-consuming and tedious, but when I finally tied the ribbon of the bonnet under my chin I judged it was worth it. I doubted if either of my ma's would recognize me.

Now I was 'In Disguise' like all the Detectives I read about.

Ping had told me to stay, but I was too jittery to sleep so I thought about what I could do.

I remembered Ping said his uncle worked at a Newspaper and that the boss might help me. Also, I remember Belle had said the Recorder's Office on A Street was opposite a Newspaper. Maybe Ping's Uncle's boss would have records and maps up there and he might even know of Belle Donne. I would go there first to do a bit of Detecting & find clews that would lead me to Belle. I would recover my Letter & take it to the Recorder's Office & collect my fortune.

Then I would buy that stagecoach ticket to Chicago & become a Detective like my pa.

That was my plan.

I slipped my medicine bag around my neck and tucked it inside the neck of the calico dress. The bell tinkled as I went out onto B Street. I locked the door behind me & slipped the key into my medicine bag and turned north. It was almost dark and the sky was that deep blue color you get sometimes on a cloudy night. It was cold and although it was not even October it smelt like snow. I thought of going back for a shawl but then I decided not to waste time. I crossed over

Taylor without incident and headed north along B.

Lively fiddle music spilled out of saloons on either side of the street. I tried not to get entranced. As I approached one saloon, the swinging wooden doors flew open & the nearest one nearly smacked me in the face. I stood back & waited for gunshots but it was just two men with cigars. They set off south along the boardwalk. As the doors of the saloon swung back & forth behind them, I glanced in. In the dim glow of oil lamps, I could see lots of men lined up at a bar & brass spittoons every so often. There were a few women in there, too, in fancy low-cut dresses. I reckoned they were Soiled Doves or Dancers.

I turned left up the steep side street called Union and then turned right on A Street, scanning the buildings right and left. It was pretty dark up here with only a few tall pitch pine torches planted in the ground beside some unoccupied hitching posts.

'Can I help you, little girl?' said a stout woman in black. She had something wrapped in newspaper under her arm. Fish, by the smell of it.

'Please, ma'am,' I said politely in a little girl voice. 'I am looking for the Newspaper across from the Recorder's Office.'

She said, 'The Territorial Enterprise is right up there on the next corner. It is that building with the flags hanging down.' She patted me on the bonnet and moved on.

Torchlight showed me a building with two limp flags on the corner of A Street and Sutton. It was a flimsy one-storey wood-frame building and as I drew closer I was able to make out a big sign that read: OFFICE OF THE

TERRITORIAL ENTERPRISE. Built up against the far side of the building was a kind of shed with a slanting tin roof and light pouring out of a window.

The light attracted me so I went there first. Peeping in the window, I saw lots of men in white shirtsleeves sitting at a long table & eating. There were bunks on either side. I thought it looked more like a boarding house than a newspaper so I went back to the main building.

The door had the words PONY EXPRESS EXTRA painted across it in big black letters. I reckoned the door needed a new coat of paint as the Pony Express had stopped bringing letters by horseback nearly a year ago when the telegraph came in.

I turned the handle and the door swung open.

A single room was lit by some coal oil lamps and warmed by a pot-bellied stove at the back. On one side of a long wooden table was the iron printing press. (I could tell because some writing on it said, WASHINGTON PRINTING PRESS.) On the other side up against the wall were some roll top desks.

There were two men in the room. One was sitting at a desk with his back to me. The other stood at the far end of the table putting little cubes in a kind of metal tray. The seated man did not turn around, but the standing man looked up. His fox-colored hair & beard were lightly powdered with pale yellow alkali dust; likewise his blue woolen shirt. He was smoking a pipe that smelled as if something had crawled in there & died. He looked more like a prospector or miner than a reporter. (I had never seen a real life reporter before, but I imagined them to be ink-stained and bespectacled.)

When the bearded man saw me, he took his foul-smelling pipe out of his mouth & said, 'I am afraid you have come to the wrong place, Miss. The nearest saloon is two doors along.'

The man in the chair looked over his shoulder at me. Seeing what he took for a little girl in a pink bonnet, he chuckled. He had a long face & sticking out ears. His black mustache & billy goat beard were neatly trimmed. He looked more like my notion of a reporter than the man with the foul-smelling pipe.

'I do not want the saloon,' I said. 'I am looking for the boss here. I have a Life or Death Problem.'

'Does your life or death problem involve a Scoop?' said the dusty man with the foul-smelling pipe. 'I am the new Local. It is my first day & I badly need a Scoop.'

I said, 'What is a Local and what is a Scoop?'

He said, 'A Local means a man who reports the local news.'

'And a Scoop?'

He said, 'It is an unpublished and startling piece of news.'

I said, 'Then, yes. I reckon I have a Scoop.'

'Please take a seat, Miss.' He stepped forward on long legs & swung a chair out from under its desk. It had little rollers on the feet & a green cushion on the walnut seat.

'My name is Sam Clemens,' he said. 'And that there is Dan De Quille, the editor of this paper. He is of no consequence. However, I will help you, if you will help me.'

LEDGER SHEET 15

THE PROSPECTOR-LOOKING REPORTER NAMED SAM
Clemens sat down opposite me.

'Tell me, little girl. What is your Life or Death Scoop?'

I sat on the chair & crossed my ankles like a well-brought up girl might do. Then I said, 'My parents were murdered and scalped and I am being pursued by a gang of desperados. I am in disguise,' I added.

The man called Dan De Quille made a kind of choking noise and swiveled around in his chair. He & Sam Clemens both stared at me with wide eyes. I was pretty sure that was Expression No. 4: Surprise. Their mouths were hanging open, too. Then Sam Clemens leaned forward & snatched my bonnet from my head. My wig came with it.

'Dang my buttons!' he exclaimed. 'You *are* in disguise. You ain't a little girl at all. You are a boy, and half Apache by the looks of you.'

'Sioux,' I said. 'I am half Sioux.'

Over at his desk, Dan De Quille chuckled. Sam Clemens narrowed his eyes at him. 'Is this some sort of prank, Dan?' he said.

Dan De Quille shrugged. 'I know nothing about it.'

Sam Clemens then rounded on me. 'Who put you up to this?' he said. 'Was it Dan over there? Or someone else?'

'I do not know what you mean,' I said, taking back my wig & bonnet. I planted them firmly on my head. 'I am in disguise for my safety. I am being pursued by a gang of desperados.'

Dan De Quille chuckled again, and turned back to his writing.

Sam Clemens did not chuckle. He narrowed his eyes at me. That was Expression No. 5. He was either mad at me, or thinking, or suspicious. Or maybe all three.

'I am not in a joking mood,' he said. 'I just arrived in Virginia City. All I know is that the streets are named after the alphabet and the atmosphere is light enough to give you a permanent nosebleed.'

'Call it "Virginia", Sam,' said Dan De Quille over his shoulder. 'Nobody calls it "Virginia City".'

Sam Clemens ignored him. 'I have just walked 70 miles through a totally uninhabited desert.'

'I doubt it,' said Dan De Quille, without turning around. 'I'll bet you hitched a lift with one of those mule trains.'

Sam Clemens said, 'I have been living on alkali water

and whang leather for the last six months.' He patted his chest so that a cloud of pale yellow dust puffed up. 'And as you can probably smell, I only had sufficient of the former for drinking purposes.'

'Beef and black coffee's what I heard,' said Dan to the wall. 'But I believe the part about you not washing for half a year.'

'I was nearly a millionaire, but for my stupidity,' said Sam Clemens, pounding the table with his hand.

'Now *that* could well be true,' said Dan with a chuckle.

'I do not have time for tomfoolery,' said Sam Clemens. 'I need a Scoop or I will have to submit this story about a passel of danged Hay Wagons.' He put his pipe in his mouth.

I said, 'My news is not tomfoolery. This afternoon my foster parents were murdered and scalped. When I found them my ma was still alive but she died soon after.'

Once again, Dan De Quille swiveled in his chair & stared at me open-eyed.

But Sam Clemens' eyes were narrowed. Expression No. 5 again. 'You do not look like a child who has just seen their parents massacred,' he said. 'You look remarkably calm.'

'That is my Thorn,' I said.

'Thorn?' said Sam Clemens.

'I cannot express emotions well. Or read them neither.'

Dan De Quille stood up and said, 'Are you a Heathen or a Believer?'

I said, 'I am a Methodist. My dead foster pa was a

Methodist preacher and I have embraced his faith.' I quoted Matthew chapter 10 & verse 32: *'Whosoever therefore shall confess me before men, him will I confess also before my Father which is in heaven.'*

Dan De Quille nodded & took a dusty black book from a shelf on his desk. He stepped closer & held it out in front of me. 'Swear on this Bible that you are not joshing us.'

I put my right hand on the Bible & said, 'I swear as God is my Witness that my parents was murdered and scalped.'

They looked at each other.

Dan De Quille said, 'Are you telling us that the Paiute Indians are up in arms? When did this happen?'

'About three hours ago at approximately 3 1/2 oclock this afternoon,' I said. 'But it was not Paiutes or any other sort of Indians. The villains who murdered my foster parents wanted people to think it was Indians. I have something they want and they are pursuing me and that is why I am in disguise.' I adjusted my bonnet to make sure it was straight.

Sam Clemens leaned towards me & gave me Expression No. 5. His narrowed eyes were a blue-green color & very shiny. 'And do you know who really did it?'

'They call him Whittlin Walt. I did not catch the names of the other two men with him.'

'Ha, ha, ha,' said Sam Clemens. 'A desperado named Whittlin Walt. That is rich. I must make a note of that in case I ever decide to write one of those Dime Novels.'

But Dan De Quille had turned white as chalk.

'What is it, Dan?' said Sam Clemens. 'What's the matter?'

Without a word, Dan De Quille stood up & went to a stack of papers on a table beside the Washington Printing Press. He took a couple of sheets from the top & handed one to me & one to Sam Clemens 'We printed up a passel of these yesterday,' he said, 'at the request of Marshal Bailey.'

In my hand I held a WANTED poster. There was a picture of a man on it. Above the picture it read: WALT DARMITAGE – ALIAS "WHITTLIN WALT". Below the picture it said, WANTED DEAD OR ALIVE. And below that it said, REWARD $2000.

For the first time I saw the face of the man who wanted me dead.

LEDGER SHEET 16

THE WANTED POSTER IN MY HANDS SHOWED AN UGLY man with pale eyes & a scar on his chin and a droopy mustache.

It chilled my blood just to look at it.

Then I noticed smaller type below the reward price.

It read as follows:

Whittlin Walt often travels with Dubois 'Extra Dub' Donahue and Boswell 'Boz' Burton. There is a reward of $200 for each of them.

'Is that him?' said Dan De Quille. 'Is that the man who murdered and scalped your parents?'

'I only saw him from up above and from a distance, but I am pretty sure this is him.'

Dan De Quille said, 'They call him "Whittlin Walt" because he likes to whittle pieces off his victims before he kills them and because he often quotes Walt Whitman as he does so.'

I said, 'Walt Whitman the poet?'

Dan De Quille nodded, 'That's right. Whittlin Walt is the most feared desperado in the Territory. He is trying to take over this whole town. It is just like him to pretend to be a Paiute to stir up trouble. People are still skittish after the Indian troubles we had two years ago.'

'Dang my buttons!' Sam Clemens put his poster on the table. 'A desperado named Whittlin Walt and his colorfully named pards strike in Virginia City. I mean Virginia. This is a Scoop, Dan. We'd better get those boys back in here and compose a new front page.'

I said, 'It wasn't here in Virginia. It was down in Temperance.'

Sam Clemens looked at Dan De Quille. 'Temperance?'

'Little two-horse hamlet down in the Carson Valley by Dayton,' said Dan De Quille. Some of the blood had returned to his face. He turned to me. 'Can you tell us what happened? Quickly and accurately?'

I told them.

They both took notes & when I finished, Dan De Quille put down his pencil & pad. He said, 'So you were the only witness?'

'Yes, sir.' I folded the WANTED poster carefully and put it in my medicine bag. I had to be able to recognize Whittlin Walt, in case I ever had the misfortune to meet him again.

Dan De Quille said, 'Does Walt know you saw him?'

I said, 'No, sir. He is after me for a Letter my parents left me.'

'Where is this Letter?'

'A Soiled Dove named Belle Donne stole it off me, along with a $20 gold coin that belonged to my ma.'

Dan De Quille's pale cheeks grew pink. 'I know Belle,' he said. 'She has a crib down on D Street and she often dines over at the Colombo Restaurant about this time of day.'

Sam Clemens looked at Dan De Quille from under his eyebrows. 'Man is the only animal that blushes,' he said. 'Or that needs to.'

Dan cleared his throat and said, 'I'd better go tell the Marshal what happened down in Temperance. We don't want to start another Indian War.' He took a plug hat from the hat tree & looked at Sam Clemens, who was beginning to rearrange the little metal letters in their tray. 'And don't you dare print that story.'

'Not print it? What do you mean?' said Sam Clemens.

Dan De Quille said, 'Whittlin Walt is the most sadistic and feared desperado we have seen in a long time. If you so much as put it in the paper that Walt knocked an old lady's prayer book from her hand he would most likely chop off your nose. Imagine what he would do if you accuse him of bloody murder. Why, he would whittle us both up for kindling!'

'But it is a Scoop, Dan,' said Sam Clemens. 'A veritable, bone fide Scoop.'

Dan De Quille looked at me. 'What is your name?'

'P.K.,' I said. 'Though my foster ma used to call me Pinky. That is short for Pinkerton.'

79

'P.K., are you certain Walt does not know you witnessed this crime?'

I said, 'I am sure. He is after me because he wants that Letter and he suspects I have it. He does not know I witnessed the crime and he does not know what I look like. But he knows I sometimes go by the name of Pinky and he knows that I am 12 years old. That is why I am in disguise.'

Dan De Quille turned to Sam Clemens & said, 'If we print that article then Walt will know that P.K. was a witness. We may as well sign this poor child's death certificate right here and now.'

LEDGER SHEET 17

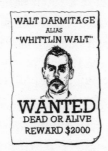

WALT DARMITAGE
ALIAS
"WHITTLIN WALT"

WANTED
DEAD OR ALIVE
REWARD $2000

DAN DE QUILLE PUT ON HIS HAT. 'I AM GOING TO tell the Marshal to ride down to Temperance and tell people there not to start another war with the Paiutes. Sam, will you stay here with P.K.? The Marshal might want to question him before he leaves. But don't you print anything until I say so.'

He hurried out of the room, closing the door behind him.

I looked at Sam Clemens & he looked at me.

Then he heaved a deep sigh & sat down. 'Well,' he said, 'as my hopes of a Scoop have been dashed upon the rocks of Prudence, I may as well try to salvage something from this wreck. Tell me about yourself. How does a pint-sized half Injun like you come to be living with a Methodist preacher and his wife?'

'My original ma was Lakota, which some people call Sioux,' I said. 'She was sent away from her tribe for taking up with a fur-trapper when she was fourteen. Later she met my pa. She liked his buttons and his beard. She fell pregnant with me and when she felt her time coming she crouched down behind a bush and out I popped. It was outside a town called Hard Luck near Mount Disappointment in the Black Hills. She named me Glares from a Bush because she said I never smiled nor cried, but just glared up at her like an evil maggot.'

Sam Clemens chuckled. 'Glares from a Bush,' he said. 'Good name. What was your ma's name? Was it something romantic, like Malaeska or Little Doe?'

'Her name was Squats on a Stump,' I said.

Sam Clemens grinned. 'And your pa?'

'His name was Pinkerton.'

Sam Clemens took the foul-smelling pipe out of his mouth. 'Allan Pinkerton? Wasn't he the man who saved President Lincoln's life last year?'

I nodded. 'He has a famous Detective Agency based out of Chicago.'

'And he's your pa?'

I shook my head. 'My pa was his elder brother Robert. He was a detective, too.'

I took the Pinkerton Rail Road Detective Button out of my medicine bag and held it out.

Sam Clemens put his pipe back in his mouth & took the button & studied it. 'Pinkerton Rail Road Detective,' he read, & then handed it back. 'I didn't know Pinkerton had an elder brother,' he said.

I said, 'Pa stayed with us for a while and then he

vamoosed. I don't even remember what he looks like. After that, my ma was left to fend for herself. In the summers we trapped animals & in the winter we lived in towns & she made Indian medicines for sick people. Then one day about two years ago she got it in her head to set out for the Washoe. I am not sure where that is.'

'That is here,' said Sam Clemens. 'It is the name of a tribe of Injuns who live in the basin valley between here and the Sierra Nevada Mountains. So your ma wanted to cash in on the Silver Boom?'

'I am not sure,' I said. 'She had a gentleman friend by then, a man named Tommy Three. Ma sold our tent & ponies and we bought places on a Wagon Train heading west. We were in Utah Territory when our wagon got separated from the rest. A band of Shoshone attacked us two days later and slaughtered my ma and Tommy Three and Hang Sung, our cook.'

Sam Clemens looked up from his notepad. 'All three massacred?'

'Yes, sir.'

'Are you joshing me?'

'No, sir, I am not.'

'Why didn't the Shoshone kill you, too, if you don't mind my asking?'

'I don't know. I can't remember what happened. I found myself sitting by the burning wagon. The Indians had taken our provisions and horses. But they left me alive with the bodies. I was wearing my old buckskins that day,' I said. 'Maybe that is why.'

'So you are a double orphan?'

I said, 'Yes, sir.'

Sam Clemens took his pipe out of his mouth and examined it. 'Then what?' he said. 'What happened after the massacre?'

'Another wagon train came along two days later,' I said. 'They found me digging the graves.'

'When was that?'

'Two years ago,' I said. 'Summer of '60.'

'First year of the Silver Boom,' said Sam Clemens. 'How old were you then?'

'I was nine years old,' I said. 'Almost ten.'

Sam Clemens put the pipe back in his mouth. 'And you were trying to bury the dead yourself?'

'Yes, sir. It would not have been right to leave Ma and Tommy Three and Hang Sung for the coyotes and buzzards. Especially Ma.'

Sam Clemens was blinking rapidly. 'Blasted alkali dust,' he said. 'Stings your eyes.' He took out a handkerchief & wiped his face. I could not see how that would help. His handkerchief was as powdered as the rest of him. After a spell he said, 'And the next wagon train took you on?'

'Yes, sir. The Reverend Emmet Jones and his wife were on that wagon train. They took pity on me and adopted me. Ma Evangeline said she had been trying to have a baby for years but the Lord had never seen fit to bless her with offspring. Pa said it was God's Will that they show me love and mercy. They were real good to me.

'We went to a place near Salt Lake City and Pa tried to preach to the Mormons. Ma taught me to read and write and Pa taught me Scripture. Half a year ago the Mormons asked Pa to move on. About the same time, the Lord told him to found a town called Temperance in the Comstock, to be an Oasis of Holiness in a Desert of Sin. We got here in the spring and now he is dead and I do not think the town of Temperance will last much longer without him.' I stared down at the floor. 'Pa used to say that Virginia City was Satan's Playground. And now it has killed him.'

Sam Clemens slowly shook his head. 'To lose two parents is a tragedy,' he said. 'But to lose four is just plain careless.'

I did not know what to say.

Sam Clemens narrowed his eyes at me. That was the fourth time he had given me Expression No. 5. 'You know,' he said, 'It is disconcerting to see what appears to be a sweet little girl talking about such things with no apparent emotions. I am not entirely sure I trust you.'

I said, 'It is my Thorn.'

He puffed his pipe for a few moments. Then he said, 'You are a strange creature, P.K.'

Without another word he stood up, reached into his pants pocket & took out a small revolver.

85

LEDGER SHEET 18

As Sam Clemens drew his small revolver, I slid under the heavy wooden table as fast as a greased snake down a gopher hole.

'Come back up, P.K.,' said Sam Clemens. 'I mean you no harm. On the contrary, I mean to do you a kindness.'

I raised my head up above the table.

'I do not believe in violence,' he said. 'I only ever shot at a man once in my life, in the first days of this War between the States we are now embroiled in. I don't know if it was my bullet that done for him or not, but it chilled me to the marrow of my bones. That is one reason I came west, to escape the carnage of that accursed War. Nonetheless, I am going to give you something that may save your life. Here. Take it.' Sam Clemens extended the revolver towards me, butt first.

Feeling sheepish, I stood up and took the gun. It was small – with a barrel only about four inches long – but it was heavy for its size. It had a walnut grip & it felt natural in my hand.

Sam Clemens said, 'That is a Smith & Wesson's number 1 seven-shooter.'

'I have heard of these,' I said. 'The ball and charge and cap are all in one cartridge.'

'That's right,' he said. 'Some people call them rimfire cartridges. That little gun is the latest thing. All you have to do is cock it & fire.'

'Where is the trigger?'

'That is called a spur trigger. When you cock the pistol it pops out.'

I flipped the barrel back on itself & took out the cylinder & saw it was loaded with seven of those new Rimfire Cartridges. I unloaded the revolver & replaced the cylinder & flipped the barrel & cocked it. Sure enough, a little trigger popped out. I tried it out a few times, pulling the trigger and hearing it go click. It looked strange, but it worked fine.

'Cunning, ain't it?' said Sam Clemens. He pulled a handful of spare cartridges from his pocket and laid them on the table.

I knew my foster pa & ma would not approve. But my Indian ma would. She had taught me to shoot a rifle & a revolver. I suspected my Detective pa would be pleased, too.

As I fed some cartridges back into the cylinder I said, '.22 caliber?'

'That's right,' he said. 'It has a ball like a homeopathic

pill and it takes all seven to make a full dose for an adult.'

I did not know what a homeopathic pill was, but a .22 caliber ball is about the smallest ball you can get.

'The other problem,' said Sam Clemens, 'is that it will not hit anything. One of my pals once fired this at a cow. As long as the cow stood still she was safe.'

I finished loading the gun & snapped the cylinder into place & looked up at him. 'If I take this, then won't you be defenseless?'

Sam Clemens sat down again & puffed on his pipe. 'I have a Colt's Navy Revolver in my bunk next door. I suppose I will have to wear it so as not to be conspicuous by its absence. I would be just as happy to give you that, but it could actually harm someone. That feeble little seven-shooter would not hurt a flea. It is just for looks.'

'So if I were to aim this gun at that picture of the mountain on the wall?' I said.

'You most likely would not hit it. But it looks good and you can scare people off with it.'

I started to put the revolver in the right hand pocket of my buckskins but quickly remembered I was wearing a pink calico dress. So I put the revolver & spare cartridges in my medicine bag. The gun's walnut grip stuck out a little. But that would make it easy to get at. I slipped the pouch under the neck of my dress. The bulge was not very noticeable.

The door opened & a boy about my age came in with a steaming pitcher. I could smell whiskey, milk, honey & nutmeg.

'The milk punch you ordered, sir,' said the boy. He had light brown hair with a cowlick, and a scattering of freckles across his nose. He put the jug down near Sam. Then he saw me & his eyes opened wide.

'Why, hello, Miss,' he said, taking off his hat & pressing it over his heart. 'I do not believe we have met.' He gave me a lopsided smile. 'Are you new in town? You are real pretty. I believe I would like to steal a kiss from you.'

'You're the Printer's Devil, ain't you?' said Sam Clemens, taking a dusty glass from a shelf.

'Yes, sir.'

'What is your name, boy?'

'Horace, sir.'

'Well, Horace,' said Sam Clemens, 'I suggest you leave your courting to another day.' He poured some of the creamy liquid into the glass. 'Now skedaddle.'

'Yes, sir,' stammered Horace. He walked towards the door. Because he was still looking at me, he bumped into it. Then he blushed & hurried out.

'What is a Printer's Devil?' I asked.

'Just another name for an apprentice printer,' said Sam Clemens. He took a sip & then smacked his lips. 'Milk punch,' he said. 'One of mankind's greatest inventions.' He drank long & deeply & when he put his glass down I saw his dusty mustache was tipped with the whiskey-tainted milk.

He was pouring himself a second glassful when the door opened & Dan De Quille came in again.

'I told the Marshal about your parents, P.K.,' he said, removing his hat and hanging it on the hat stand. 'He and his Deputy are on their way down to Temperance right now. I looked in at the Colombo Restaurant but Belle was not there.'

He pulled up a chair and said, 'You say Belle took your letter, the one Walt and his pards were after?'

'Yes, sir,' I said.

'Can you remember what that letter said?'

'I can remember exactly what it said. You show me something once, I never forget it.'

THE OTHER WANTED POSTER OF WHITTLIN WALT
lay face up on the table. Dan De Quille turned it over
and pushed a pencil towards me.

'Write down as much about that letter as you can
remember,' he said. 'We have got to figure out why Walt
wants that document so badly. Sam,' he said, 'pour me a
mug of that punch. I could use a stiff drink.'

While the two reporters drank Milk Punch, I
reproduced the Letter as faithfully as I could. I even
added the illegible signature and my pa's witness. Then
I slid it over for them to inspect.

Dan De Quille and Sam Clemens both bent their
heads over my reproduction of the Letter.

After a while Dan looked up at me. 'Well, P.K.,' he
said. 'I am not sure, but if your letter is genuine and if
you can recover it, then you might have a claim to part
of Mount Davidson. That would make you owner of half

the mines here in Virginia. You could be a millionaire.'

Sam Clemens choked on his milk punch & some of it spurted out his nose. Dan De Quille patted him on the back. A cloud of pale yellow alkali dust puffed up. 'Sam,' said he. 'Go take a bath. Your story about the hay wagons will do for today, I think.'

'A millionaire?' said Sam Clemens, dabbing his face with his dusty handkerchief. 'This calico-clad Injun could be a millionaire?'

'Selfridge and Bach's Bath House down on B Street is good,' said Dan De Quille. 'The water is hot and changed fairly frequently. They are open until midnight. Tell Bach to burn the clothes you are wearing now.'

Sam Clemens looked down at his dusty limbs. Then he scratched his armpit. 'You are probably right. I do believe I am lousy. But this is all I've got to wear,' he said. He looked at me. 'Maybe the millionaire will loan me a dollar or two?'

Dan De Quille sighed & stood up. He reached into his pocket & flipped Sam Clemens a gold coin. 'There is twenty dollars,' he said. 'Bach will give you something to wear. Claim a bunk in the shed next door. You can pay me back when you get your first week's wages.'

Sam Clemens nodded. 'That is a good plan.' He stuck his pipe in his mouth & strode on long legs to the door.

Just before he went out he turned & said to me, 'I hope it works out for you, P.K. I seldom pray, but I believe I will make an exception in your case.'

'Thank you, sir,' I said. 'And thank you for the seven-shooter.'

When the door closed behind him Dan De Quille turned to look at me. 'Seven-shooter?'

'Yes, sir. Mr. Sam Clemens kindly gave me his Smith & Wesson's number 1 seven-shooter. It is the latest thing with the ball and charge and cap all packed together in a metal cartridge.'

'Do you know how to operate a fire-arm?'

'Yes, sir. I know how to shoot a gun.'

'Probably not a bad idea, then,' said Dan De Quille. 'Everybody in this town packs a piece of some sort.' He patted the Colt's Navy Revolver in his own belt. Then he sat down & studied my Letter again. 'P.K.,' he said, 'have you ever heard the name Grosh?'

'No, sir,' I said. And then a thought struck me. 'Do you think that could be the last name of the man who wrote the Letter? Whose signature I could not decipher?'

'I do,' said Dan De Quille. 'Here in Virginia the name Grosh is legendary. Hosea Ballou Grosh and Ethan Allen Grosh were brothers. They had been over in California at a place called Volcano. They were mining experts who came here about ten years ago to look for silver. Silver, do you hear me? Not gold.'

'Silver,' I repeated.

'That is correct,' said Dan De Quille. 'Now there were already some miners here. They were spillovers from the Big California Gold Rush of '49. They made a little money by placer mining but when they tried to dig they found only a heavy blue mud. Those miners cursed it, but the Grosh Brothers realized that blue mud contained *silver*.

In 1856 they wrote to their father back east that they had found rich ledges of silver up in Gold Canyon and that one of those ledges was a "perfect monster".'

'Is that good?' I asked.

'That is very good,' said Dan De Quille. 'The Grosh Brothers were on the brink of becoming fabulously rich. But they died before they could stake their claim.'

At that moment the door of the Territorial Enterprise swung open with a bang as loud as a gunshot. Dan and I both jumped up out of our chairs.

It was not Whittlin Walt at the door, but a smiling Chinaman in loose blue pantaloons and shirt like Ping's.

'Hello, Joe,' said Dan De Quille. And to me he said, 'Old Joe here is our cook. Most of the boys eat next door but he sometimes brings me a special dinner.'

I nodded a greeting. This must be Ping's uncle.

'Hello, Mister Dan,' said Old Joe. 'You hungry? You want special dinner?'

'I am ravenous,' said Dan De Quille. 'I could eat an entire steer, horns and all. How about you, P.K.?'

'Yes, sir,' I replied. 'I am ravenous, too.'

'We have no steer tonight,' said Old Joe. 'Them boys ate it, horns and all.'

Dan grinned. 'Well then, how about one of your late night breakfasts?' He turned to me. 'What'll you have to drink? Milk? Sarsaparilla? Whiskey?'

'I am partial to black coffee,' I said.

Dan De Quille nodded & turned to Old Joe. 'Two coffees,' he said. 'And bring us a stack of pancakes and bacon with some of that good maple syrup. Not the sorghum syrup, Joe. The maple syrup.'

Old Joe bowed, and when he turned to go, I saw he had a gray pigtail so long that it reached past his waist.

Dan De Quille said to me, 'Where was I?'

'The Grosh Brothers and their monster ledge of silver,' I said.

'That's right. Well, the Grosh Brothers tested this monster vein and they found it to be beautifully soft and untainted by other metals. But to get out the silver, they needed money.'

Dan sat back & smiled. 'There is a famous saying hereabouts. *You need a gold mine to afford a silver mine.* So they determined to go back to Volcano and get some financial backers. But before they could leave Hosea put a pickaxe through his foot. Sadly, the wound festered and he died in September. Ethan was grief-stricken and tempted to give up. He rallied his spirits and decided to stay on and mine that monster vein of silver, but first he had to bury his brother.'

I nodded again & thought of my dead foster parents, lying scalped & unburied. I hoped the Marshal would take care of their bodies.

Dan De Quille said, 'By the time he had paid off the expenses of his brother's burial, it was mid-November. They say you should never cross the Sierra Nevada mountains after October. Ethan Allen Grosh and his companion – a young Canadian called Bucke – took a gamble in crossing the mountains so late in the season.'

Dan shook his head. 'Their gamble did not pay off.'

I sat forward. I had heard the terrible tale of a family called Donner who had been caught in a blizzard in those same mountains. Some had died of hunger & the others had only survived by eating the frozen bodies of their companions.

'Was he froze in a blizzard and eaten by his companion?' I said.

'No, but they were caught in a heavy snowfall and they did have to eat their donkey. They threw away all their belongings, including maps, claims and samples. By the time they reached the Last Chance Mining Camp, their feet were so badly frozen that they had to be amputated.'

I shuddered. I knew amputation was when they cut parts off of you.

I tried to imagine having no feet.

I could not do it.

'Bucke survived,' said Dan De Quille, 'but poor Ethan Allen died. There is a rumor that he wrote a Deed for that monster silver vein on his deathbed. When Bucke recovered, he searched but could not find it anywhere. Still, there were other people there in the Last Chance Mining Camp. Perhaps one of them took it. Ethan Allen Grosh's lost Deed is the Holy Grail of this region. Anyone who finds it and presents it would be rich as Creesus.'

'**What is a Holy Grail?**' I asked. '**And who is** Creesus?'

'A Holy Grail is an Object of Great Desire. And Creesus was the richest fellow who ever lived.' Dan De Quille stood up. 'Your stolen document claims the land north of the Divide and south of the Stream on Sun Peak near Pleasant Town.' He pointed at a picture on the wall. 'This is a Panoramic View of Virginia City done just last year. Sun Peak is the former name of Mount Davidson, to whose side we are clinging at this very moment.'

'And Pleasant Town?'

'Virginia City is Pleasant Town,' said Dan. 'It got its new name two years ago when a drunken miner named "Old Virginny" Finney fell and broke a bottle of whiskey on a rock. Not wanting that whiskey to go to waste, he christened this place Old Virginny, after himself. This amused the locals and the name Virginia stuck.'

'Like Dayton,' I said. 'Which used to be known as Chinatown.'

Dan nodded. 'The fact that your missing document names "Sun Peak" and "Pleasant Town" rather than "Mount Davidson" and "Virginia City" indicates that it may well be genuine.'

'What else would it be?' I said.

'A clever forgery.'

At that moment, the door swung open with a crash. We both started.

Old Joe the Chinaman came in with a tray.

'Dang it all, Joe,' said Dan. 'Don't fling open the door like that.'

'Beg pardon, Mister Dan,' said Old Joe. He put the tray on the long table & took off 2 plates of pancakes & a jug of syrup & 2 mugs of black coffee. There was also a dish of yellow butter – molded into the shape of a dragon – and some cutlery.

'Bring me some cream for my coffee, Joe,' said Dan De Quille as Old Joe went out. 'You never remember my cream.'

'Chop, chop!' said Old Joe, and hurried out.

'Tuck in, P.K.,' said Dan De Quille. 'But watch out for the butter. Joe likes to mold it in pretty shapes, but he often gets mouse hairs and bugs and other trash in there.'

I was hungry & the pancakes were delicious. There were not too many hairs in the butter.

'This reminds me,' said Dan, as he poured maple syrup onto his stack of pancakes. 'There is a rumor that Old Pancake himself befriended the Grosh brothers, in order to discover their secret. Some even say they made him a partner.'

'Who is Old Pancake?' I asked.

'Why, Old Pancake is Henry Comstock,' said Dan. 'He gave his name to the Ledge we are sitting on, though whether there is one single ledge or many is a moot point. Old Pancake barged in on two other miners who had just discovered a lead. He cut an impressive figure in his store-bought suit and when he claimed the land was his, they believed him. Now the whole mother lode is named after him.'

'Why do people call him "Old Pancake"?' I asked.

Dan chuckled. 'They say he was too lazy to bake bread from his flour and so he always made pancakes.'

I said, 'Or maybe he just liked pancakes better than bread, like me. On special days, Ma Evangeline always makes...' I trailed off and stared at the floor. For a moment I had forgotten about my dear foster ma lying dead on the floor of our cabin. I would never eat her pan-cakes again.

We ate in silence for a few minutes, then Dan De Quille picked up the WANTED poster with my replica on the back & frowned. 'You know,' he said. 'One thing about that document puzzles me.'

'What is that?'

'I find it strange that Ethan Allen Grosh would bequeath all his land to "The Bearer" and not to his father back east or to any of his partners in Volcano or even to Bucke, his companion.'

I said, 'Maybe my pa was one of those people in the

Last Chance Mining Camp and maybe he helped Ethan Allen Grosh and he wanted to thank my pa. And maybe Pa told him to make it out to "The Bearer" because he planned to send it to me and my ma, so we would not be poor any more.'

'Maybe.' Dan put the WANTED poster back on the table, face up. 'Whatever the reason,' he said, mopping up the last of his maple syrup with his final forkful of pancake, 'I believe the first person to present that document at the Recorder's Office could have a claim to half this mountain and the silver in it. No wonder Walt wants it so badly.'

'What if Belle were to take that letter to the Recorder's Office?' I asked.

Dan De Quille shrugged. 'Then the fortune would be hers.'

'But that Letter is mine,' I said.

'Then you'd better get it back before tomorrow morning,' said Dan.

For a third time that evening, the door burst open with a bang.

Dan De Quille sighed deeply & said, 'Joe, I told you not to fling open that door.'

Then I saw his eyes grow wide as he stared over my shoulder. I turned slowly to see a blood-chilling sight.

This time it *was* Whittlin Walt. And his two ugly pards were with him.

WHITTLIN WALT STOOD IN THE DOORWAY LOOKING in & for the first time I saw his face properly. He did not have the droopy mustache from the WANTED poster on the table before me, but I recognized him anyway from the powerful smell of Bay Rum Hair Tonic that pervaded the room. He had icy blue eyes & a broken nose & a scar across his chin. His long biscuit-colored coat did not quite hide a special belt with two holsters: one for his bone-handled Colt's Army Revolver & another for his big Bowie Knife. I could not be sure, but I thought I saw two bloody scalps hanging from his belt.

Walt stepped into the lamplit room & I could hear his spurs jingle as he moved. His pards followed close behind. One was tall & scrawny with the biggest Adam's apple I have ever seen. I learned later that he was Dubois 'Extra Dub' Donahue. The short one with the squinty left eye & busted nose was whiny-voiced Boswell 'Boz'

Burton, the villain who had chased me & Belle through Chinatown.

Would he recognize me in my disguise as a prim and proper girl?

I looked at Dan and saw his gaze flicking from Walt to the WANTED poster and back.

I put my plate down on top of the poster, so that Walt would not see it.

This seemed to snap Dan De Quille out of his trance. He stood up & said, 'May I help you fellows?' He sounded calm, but I was close enough to hear him swallow hard.

'Yeah,' said Walt. He was chewing tobacco. 'We want to report a crime. Some Injuns kilt the preacher down in Temperance. Kilt his wife, too. Scalped 'em both.'

'Crimes should be reported at the Marshal's Office,' said Dan De Quille. His fingertips were resting lightly on the table & I noticed they were trembling.

'Marshal ain't there,' said Walt. 'Nor his Deputy neither. Just a note says they've gone out.' Walt spat a stream of tobacco-stained saliva onto the floor.

'Then you should go see the Sheriff in Gold Hill,' said Dan.

'We wanted to give you a chance to publish this tragic news first. Ain't you interested? Shall we take it to the newspaper down in Carson?'

'Of course we're interested,' stammered Dan. 'Come in.' Then he looked down at me. 'Maisie,' he said. 'You'd best get home now or your mother will be worried.'

I nodded & stood up.

'In return for our news,' said Walt, 'we were hoping you might give us some information.'

'Information?' said Dan. With trembling hands, he put his plate on top of mine & picked them both up & held them out to me. He had scooped up the WANTED poster with the plates, like a place mat.

Walt said, 'We are looking for the preacher's kid, a twelve-year-old half Injun who goes by the name of Pinky. You seen anyone like that around here?'

'No,' stammered Dan. 'I have not seen a twelve-year-old half Injun called Pinky.' To me he said, 'Tell your mother the dinner was delicious. Now run along home.' Then he patted the top of my bonnet.

I held the WANTED poster up against the bottom of the plates as I took them from Dan. Then I walked steadily towards Walt & his pards, keeping my bonnet down.

'The kid we are looking for,' said Boz, 'has cold black eyes and a muddy complexion. He smashed me in the face with a cold flat iron. He is about the same height as your little girl there.'

I froze.

Dan said, 'I have not seen him.' But his voice was shaky.

I resumed walking towards the door. The sides of my bonnet were like the blinkers horses sometimes wear: they kept me from getting spooked by the beady eyes of the three desperados scrutinizing me.

All I could see of them was their legs. I prayed that those legs would carry their owners away. Sure enough, they began to move aside to let me pass.

But then, just when I thought I was out of it, a spurred boot came out to block my path. A whiny, nasal voice said, 'Just a minute, little girl.'

I knew the boot belonged to Boz, whose nose I had broken. I knew if I looked up at him he would recognize my 'cold black eyes' and my 'muddy complexion'.

So I threw down the plates and ran for it.

I heard a shout. 'After her, boys!'

Their spurred boots sounded like gunshots on the boardwalk behind me.

Then I heard a bullet whizz past my ear & realized they really *were* gunshots.

EVEN AT NIGHT THE STREETS OF VIRGINIA ARE BUSY.

As I sped across Sutton without looking left or right, I nearly got trampled by a two-horse buggy. The horses reared and pawed the air only inches from my head.

But I had only one thought, 'I must get away from those bullets!'

I turned to head south on B Street.

As I rounded the corner at a run, I saw open double doors and light pouring out.

I charged inside and up some carpeted stairs, then left along a corridor with numbered rooms on both sides.

I thought, 'This must be a hotel.'

I could hear spurred boots jangling up the stairs behind me, so I began to try the doors.

I found one unlocked & flung it open & ran through a dimly-lit room.

Out of the corner of my eye I saw a woman in a puffy

lime-green dress and a man in a brocade waistcoat. They were bouncing up and down on the bed. Ma Evangeline would not have approved. She always rebukes me when I jump up and down on a mattress. She says it is hard on the bed-frame.

'Hey!' said the man & the woman squealed, 'Oh! A little girl!'

I ignored them & charged straight through some double glass doors before me. I had a good head of steam going and caught myself just before I plunged over the rail of a balcony & onto some horses tied to the hitching post below. I staggered back and looked around. There was another balcony over on the building to my right, but there was a fair-sized gap between the two balconies and a drop of about twenty feet. I would have to jump that gap if I wanted to escape being shot.

Cursing my little white boots and wishing I had my moccasins, I clambered up onto the rail. For a moment I teetered. Then I found my balance. Then I jumped.

I landed on the other balcony awkwardly, slightly twisting my right ankle.

'Dang it!' I said, as I limped to the glass doors. Thankfully they were unlocked. They opened into a dark room with a thread of light on the far side, marking the bottom of an inner door. I could hear the muffled sound of a hurdy gurdy playing 'Aura Lee'. I ran across the dark room and as I opened the far door I sent up a prayer of thanks and also of petition. 'Help me, Lord,' I prayed. 'Oh, help me escape these desperados!'

The sound of the hurdy gurdy grew louder as I stepped out on a wooden walkway.

I could smell whiskey and cigar smoke. That, and the jolly music, told me I was in a saloon.

I went to the rail of the walkway and looked down on a big, brightly lit room. There were lots of round green tables and men sitting at them playing cards. There was a long mahogany bar at one end of the room and a Negro hurdy gurdy player and some half dressed ladies at the other.

I stood there for a moment, looking for an escape route. Then I saw some stairs to my left.

As I turned to go towards them I saw Walt coming up.

As I turned to go right, a door opened & Extra Dub stepped out.

They were both smiling at me and they were taking their time.

They knew they had me trapped.

'Well, well, well,' said Walt. 'You must be Pinky. Looks like I have got the bulge on you. Give me that Letter and you will come to no harm.'

'I don't have it,' I said. 'A Soiled Dove stole it off me. A Soiled Dove by the name of Belle Donne.'

Walt had reached my level. 'Tell us another story like that,' he said, cocking his revolver, 'and I will fill you full of lead.'

I looked over the railing of the walkway to the room below. Directly underneath me was a round green table. The men sitting around it were looking up at me. There was a pile of coins in the middle of the table & some drinks & some playing cards.

On my left, Whittlin Walt was drawing a bead on me & on my right Extra Dub was taking careful aim, too.

I did not have many options.

In fact, it seemed to me there was only one.

I vaulted over the railing down onto the table below.

A moment after I leapt, twin shots rang out.

I was expecting to crash down on the table & you can imagine my surprise when I found myself safe in a man's strong arms. One of the gamblers had got to his feet and caught me. Thanks to his quick reflexes, I had escaped being shot or bruised.

The gambler and I stared into each other's eyes. His were so dark they were almost black. He showed no emotion.

The hurdy gurdy player had stopped playing and for a moment everything was silent, apart from the dying echo of the gunshots.

Then from the walkway above came Walt's harsh voice. 'Dub, you Fool! You creased me! Don't aim at me! Aim at her!'

More gunshots rang out & some women started screaming & I found myself set on my feet as my rescuer took out his own piece & commenced firing up at the men in the gallery. A moment later everyone else had their guns out & blazing, too.

As far as I could tell it was a Free For All.

I did not linger to see the outcome.

Quick as a telegram I ran underneath the walkway to the bar and hurried along behind it at a crouch. It formed a useful barrier between me and the flying balls of lead.

When I got to the end of the bar nearest the door I paused, straightened my bonnet, took a deep breath and then charged the swinging saloon doors with my arms stuck out stiff before me.

As Providence would have it, the left-hand door smacked a man in the face as he was running in. He crashed backwards onto the boardwalk, out cold. The flickering torchlight showed me that it was Walt's broken-nosed pard: the unlucky Boz.

For the second time that day I had smashed him in the face.

I could hear gunfire coming from the saloon but nobody had yet burst out after me. I tipped my head down and limped along the torchlit street as quickly as I dared, not wanting to attract the attention of the people hurrying this way.

Keeping to the shadows on the west side of B Street, I walked faster and faster until soon I was running. I sped across one of those steep side streets, looking neither right nor left.

I was lucky not to be run over by a cart or buggy. I was in such a daze that I trampled on the tail of an old brown dog sprawled on the boardwalk just past the Old Corner Saloon. He uttered a shrill yap and then leapt to his feet and started to bark. The poor creature had been minding his own business chewing a bone in front of a shuttered-up meat market when I trod on his tail.

That dog's yelp brought me to my senses.

I slowed to a walk again but as I crossed another steep side street I realized that if I kept on going I would probably leave the shelter of the town behind. I stopped and backed up against a rough plank wall beside a barrel. I suddenly felt exhausted & confused. I was shivering, too, for it had begun to snow. I did not have a cloak or a coat over my thin calico dress.

A few hours ago I had possessed a Letter that might have made me a Millionaire. Now I was standing in the middle of a strange and sinful town, with three murderous desperados on my trail. To add insult to injury, I was wearing little white boots, a bonnet, a pink dress and bloomers underneath.

'Please, Lord, help,' I prayed.

Then I lifted up my eyes and at once 2 Solutions presented themselves to me.

Across the street I saw a torchlit sign that was as welcome as a watering hole in the desert. It said, Isaiah Coffin's Ambrotype & Photographic Gallery.

I had the key to that Safe Haven in my medicine pouch. I thought of the warm buffalo skin and the soft couch. How I longed to be safely wrapped up in the one & lying on the other.

But another sign just two doors along read: COLOMBO RESTAURANT – Titus Jepson Proprietor, Private Room for Ladies & Children.

The Colombo Restaurant was the name of the place where Belle Donne sometimes took her meals.

I could either use my key to take shelter in the Photographic Gallery and lie low till morning as Ping had recommended, or I could continue my search for Belle Donne and my purloined Letter.

I decided to be brave and pursue my Quest for that Letter. But first I had to do one important thing in Isaiah Coffin's Ambrotype & Photographic Gallery.

Get out of those girly clothes.

OIL LAMPS ON THE TABLES & WALLS GAVE THE DINING room of the Colombo Restaurant a pleasing golden glow. It smelled of cabbage & roast pork & also of wood smoke from the cherry-ripe cast-iron stove in one corner. The room was full of tables & every seat was occupied. Most of the men were bearded. There was a comforting sound of cutlery on china when I first entered, but then it grew quiet as the diners stopped eating & turned to stare at me.

I had changed into a new outfit.

I thought, 'Maybe they don't serve people dressed like this at the Colombo Restaurant.'

My suspicion was confirmed when a Mexican boy carrying empty plates stood before me.

'Get out!' he said. 'Chop, chop! You can't come in here!' He made a flapping motion at me with his free hand.

I stood firm and in a low voice I said, 'I am looking for Belle Donne. I have an important message for her.'

The young waiter stared hard at me for a few moments, glanced around at the diners, then nodded. 'Follow me,' he said. 'We have a special room for women and children.' Then he added in a low voice. 'Next time you come here, use the side entrance by the privy.'

I followed him across the crowded dining room and through a door into another smaller dining room, also lit by a few oil lamps & warmed by a wood-burning stove. There was a family of six at a rectangular table & a woman in black who sat alone at a small round table.

Still holding the dishes, the young waiter showed me to a small square table in one corner by an east-facing window & a potted fern. It was warm in there & I sat down gratefully.

The young waiter said, 'Wait here. I will get the proprietor and owner, Mr. Titus Jepson.'

A moment later he returned. 'Mr. Jepson says that any friend of Belle's is a friend of his. What would you like to eat?'

'I have just eaten,' I said. 'But I am partial to black coffee.'

The waiter nodded. 'Coming right up.'

While I waited, I studied the other people in the dining room. The blond family were talking to each other in a foreign language. They looked & sounded like Olaf, the bully from Temperance. From this I deduced they were Swedish. They were of solid build & had heads shaped like dice.

The woman in the corner reminded me of my teacher

in Dayton, Miss Marlowe. But Miss Marlowe is pretty & this lady was plain. She was crinkling her nose at me to make Expression No. 3: Disgust.

The kitchen door opened & a redheaded man poked his head out & looked at me for a while. Then he retreated.

A few minutes later the redheaded man reappeared with a wedge of white-frosted chocolate cake and a thick china mug of black coffee. He put them both on the table and then took a seat opposite me.

'My name is Titus Jepson,' he said. 'Owner and proprietor of this establishment.'

He was plump and wore a greasy white apron. From these clews I guessed he was the chief cook as well. 'Gus tells me you're American,' he said. 'In spite of your get up. And that you know Belle?'

I nodded and looked down at the piece of cake.

It looked good.

It made me think of the cake sitting at home. The cake with the chocolate frosting & licorice writing that Ma Evangeline had baked. My birthday cake that nobody would eat. I could hardly believe it was still my birthday. In the past four hours I had witnessed my foster parents' death & rid on top of a stagecoach & hid under the skirts of a Soiled Dove & been robbed & been shot at, too.

'Go on and have some,' said Titus Jepson. 'The cake is on the house. Like I told Gus, a friend of Belle's is a friend of mine.'

I took a forkful and lifted it to my mouth. Then I hesitated.

What if Titus Jepson was in cahoots with Walt and knew who I was?

What if the cake was poisoned?

Had I learned nothing from my four hours in Satan's Playground?

I lowered my fork.

'Don't you like chocolate?' said Titus Jepson.

'I love chocolate.'

'Then why don't you eat it?'

I said, 'I am afraid it might be poisoned.'

Titus Jepson chuckled. 'That cake ain't poisoned and I'll prove it.' He pinched off a portion and ate it. 'That there's my special Comstock layer cake. Chocolate with a ledge of silver frosting.' He grinned & showed a missing front tooth. 'Course the frosting's not really silver. It's icing sugar flavored with vanilla, you bet.'

I took a bite.

It was delicious.

Maybe even better than Ma Evangeline's cake.

Titus Jepson said, 'The frosting is supposed to represent the silver under the mountain. You can probably guess that I am a Uniledgarian.'

I said, 'Beg pardon?'

He said, 'A Uniledgarian is a person who believes in One-Ledge.'

'Everybody talks about "ledges",' said I, taking another bite. 'But I don't understand what a ledge is.'

'Why, a ledge is a vein of silver, only it's more like a sheet than a vein. Some people around here adhere to the

---

115

doctrine of multiple ledges, like a little stack of pancakes that have fallen over. But most of us believe there is one single ledge under this town, like the frosting in your cake.' Titus Jepson pointed a chubby finger at my cake & he said. 'May I?'

I did not know what he meant so I said, 'Yes?'

Titus Jepson made his right hand into a fist & shmooshed my piece of chocolate cake.

I looked at the shmooshed cake in dismay. I had been enjoying it.

I said, 'You shmooshed my cake.'

Titus Jepson said, 'Imagine that cake is the mountain. Mount Davidson.'

I said, 'I was enjoying that piece of cake.'

'I'm glad to hear that,' he said. 'Now, imagine that the vanilla frosting is a big deposit of silver ore.' He took my butter knife & scraped the frosting off the top & put it on one side of the plate. 'Not that top frosting. The frosting inside. The frosting *between* the layers. That is the ledge, the Mother Lode.'

I nodded.

'Of course that silver is mixed with quartz and other trash, and you have to pound it and treat it and amalgamate it before it becomes silver, but it's there.'

I looked at my piece of cake & nodded again.

'See how the frosting between the layers is thin in some places but thick in others? Because I shmooshed it?'

I nodded.

'And see how even though it's all shmooshed around it is still connected, despite the various dips, angles, spurs and variations?' He held up the plate & showed me. 'Still connected, do you see?'

I did not understand all his words, but I clearly saw what he meant.

'Yes,' I said.

Titus Jepson put down the plate & picked up the knife. He used it to make three small dents in the top of the shmooshed cake. 'These are various ravines in Mount Davidson,' he said. 'That one is the Ophir Ravine.' Then he took my coffee cup & poured a little dribble of coffee on it. 'And that there is a little stream that trickles down through the Ophir Ravine. It is called the Mexican Stream because in the early days of this city two poor Mexican brothers lived there and the stream was on their property. They traded their water for a few feet of a mine called the Ophir and they called their section of the ledge the Mexican Mine. It turned out to be the thickest part of the frosting ledge. Those two poor brothers sold it a few years later and now they both have mansions, you bet.'

Titus Jepson picked up a knife & carefully cut a small section out of my cake, then held it up on the knife. 'I own three feet of the Mexican Mine and it provides some mighty tasty income.' He popped the segment of cake in his mouth & ate it.

I also took a bite.

'Sorry I shmooshed your cake,' said Titus Jepson.

'Would you like a fresh piece?'

'No, sir,' I said, taking a forkful of the Mother Lode. 'It is just as good shmooshed as it is puffy. And now I understand what a ledge is.'

Titus Jepson nodded and smiled. 'Now that I have told you something, you can tell me something in return. What has Belle done now?'

I guess I should have figured.

In return for a piece of Comstock Layer Cake – and a lesson on the geography of the region – Titus Jepson wanted information about Belle Donne.

'Is Belle your daughter?' I asked.

Titus Jepson looked at me with Expression No. 4: Surprise. 'Dog my cats, no! She is going to be my wife.'

'Your wife?'

'I hope so. I want to make an honest woman of her and marry her,' he said. Then he looked down at the table and scraped at a bit of dried egg with his thumbnail. 'But she has a bad habit,' he said.

I said, 'I crack my knuckles sometimes. Ma Evangeline says that is a bad habit.'

Titus Jepson shook his head & looked up at me. I saw that his eyes were moist. 'Not that kind of habit,' he said. 'I'm afraid she is in danger of becoming a Dope Fiend.'

'What is a Dope Fiend?' I asked.

'Opium Smoker,' said Titus Jepson. 'Every time Belle gets a few dollars she goes down there to Chinatown and has a pipe. I have tried to get her to quit but it is no good. I don't think she'll ever change.'

I nodded wisely. Ma Evangeline always told Pa Emmet that his pipe was a bad habit.

At that moment we heard a commotion from the room next door.

'Where is she?' yelled a voice, muffled by the door between us. 'When I find her, I am going to gut her like a pig.'

I choked on my mouthful of cake.

Whittlin Walt had found me once again.

BEFORE I COULD BOLT FOR THE EXIT, THE DOOR OF the Private Room for Ladies & Children burst open & in came Whittlin Walt & his pards.

Luckily, I had stopped by Isaiah Coffin's Ambrotype & Photographic Gallery before coming to the restaurant and I had adopted a new disguise, that of a Celestial. I was wearing loose blue pantaloons and a shirt with toggle buttons and also a flat straw hat with a false pigtail attached. I had looked myself over in the mirror and I judged that my 'muddy complexion' and slanting 'cold black eyes' made this my most convincing disguise so far.

Walt would not give me a second glance. He was looking for a little girl in pink calico and a bonnet.

Or was he?

'Where is she?' yelled Walt again. He was waving a Bowie Knife as long as my forearm. 'Where is Belle

Donne? They said she would be here!'

'Oh!' cried Titus Jepson, jumping up from my table. 'Oh my!'

'You!' said Walt, grasping a fistful of Jepson's apron and pulling him close. 'Where is Belle Donne? They told me she eats here regular.'

'I don't know!' cried Titus Jepson.

'Do you know who I am?' said Walt.

'No,' stammered Titus Jepson.

'My name is Whittlin Walt. You tell me where to find that girl or I will start cutting off your fingers and toes!'

'No,' said Titus Jepson. 'Please, no. I'm very attached to my digits. I don't know where Belle is. I swear!'

The Mexican waiter was standing to one side watching. He was clenching & unclenching his fists. The blond family and the woman in black were staring wide-eyed.

'Talk!' said Walt. He grabbed Titus Jepson by the wrist & pulled him over to my table, which was the nearest. I shrank back against the wall. Walt pushed Jepson's plump hand flat on the tabletop & brought down his Bowie Knife.

Titus Jepson screamed as the tip of his left pinkie finger flew up into the air. It dropped down onto my plate, right among the crumbs and frosting.

The woman in black began to scream & the blond children were crying.

A pool of blood was spreading on the table.

'Now talk!' said Walt, holding up his bloody Bowie

Knife. 'Or I will keep whittling away at you and finally: *I will show you that nothin can happen more beautiful than death.*' He laughed, as if he had said something funny.

'I'll talk!' screamed Titus Jepson. 'I'll talk!'

'Where is Belle?'

'She is probably down in one of them Opium Dens in Chinatown.'

'Which one?' said Walt letting his knife hover over the ring-finger of Jepson's left hand.

'Ah Sing!' said Titus Jepson. 'She usually goes to Ah Sing.'

'I know Ah Sing,' said Extra Dub. 'It is down there on F Street. Little coyote hole in the mountain.'

Walt nodded and spat some tobacco juice onto the floor. 'See?' he said. 'That wasn't so hard, was it?' He wiped his knife on the seat of his pants and said to his pards, 'Come on, boys. Let's pay a visit to Chinatown.'

'No!' sobbed Titus Jepson. 'Don't hurt Belle. Please don't hurt my Belle.'

But they were already heading out the side door.

As they left, Extra Dub pointed his Colt's Navy Revolver at the ceiling and fired a shot. Its loud report made my ears ring & caused flakes of plaster to rain down on us. It set off a new wave of screaming.

Titus Jepson was gasping & weeping & shaking his head. 'Oh no!' he cried. 'They'll carve her up. My poor Belle.'

I stood up.

So far Walt and his pards had called the shots.

It was time for me to do something apart from running away.

'Don't worry,' I said to Titus Jepson. 'I will find Belle first and I will warn her.'

Titus Jepson looked down at me with a blotched and tearful face.

'If you help Belle,' he said. 'I will give you discounted meals here till the end of time.'

LEDGER SHEET 25

I DID NOT NEED MY INDIAN TRACKING SKILLS TO
follow the trail of Walt and his pards. A light dusting of
snow showed their tracks as plain as day. I soon caught
up with them at the junction of Taylor and D Street. I
kept them in sight but hung back in the shadows cast by
the torches.

They had picked up a bottle of whiskey somewhere
and were taking swigs from it in turn. Once Boz slipped
and fell. Walt reached out a hand as if to help but only
took the bottle. Extra Dub helped Boz up and they all
laughed.

I had to be careful, too. The snow made the steep road
real slippery and I was not used to wooden-soled sandals.

By-and-by Walt and his pards turned left at F Street,
the same street where I had found myself a few hours
before. Chinatown looked different at night. A fog of
incense hung over the huts and paper lanterns glowed

like stars. I took my seven-shooter out of my medicine bag and held it in my right hand. Then I slipped my right hand into the sleeve of my left arm and vice versa, as I had seen some Celestials do. That meant my gun was ready but hidden, and my hands were not too cold. Once Boz turned to look back, but I just kept my head down and he did not seem concerned. I guessed I looked just like another Chinese boy to him.

Extra Dub seemed to know the way and he led Walt and Boz through a warren of shacks and tents. At last they reached a part of the snow-dusted hillside with a rock-lined cut leading to a low wooden door.

'You keep watch, Dub,' I heard Walt say. 'Boz and I will have a look inside.'

Walt and Boz had to bow their heads to enter. Dub took a cigar from his coat pocket & struck a match against the rough stone of the cut. As he bent his head to light his smoke, I pulled my hat down & put my sleeves together & I shuffled past him.

Dub did not give me a second glance.

The wooden door opened as silently as if its hinges sat in cups of oil. As I went in I saw the wooden lintel above me was blackened by smoke. Inside, it was so dim and smoky that at first I could only see a few globes of yellow, red or blue light. It was quiet in there, too, and apart from the soft chink of the desperados' spurs and a strange bubbling I could hear nothing. There were people smoking in there and the bittersweet tobacco smelled like burning flowers and made me dizzy. I knew that was the Opium Smoke. I tried to breathe through my mouth, so I would not become a Dope Fiend.

As my eyes adjusted, I could see that the walls of this cave were lined with narrow bunk beds stacked four high. Almost every bunk was occupied by a person sleeping or smoking. The pipes were very long and I guessed they were Chinese, like the tobacco. Some of the pipes were so long that they had to be held by attendants dressed just like me.

I heard Walt talking and turned to see him looming over a little old Chinaman who sat at a table inside the door. On this table were brass scales & boxes & coins.

Walt was speaking to the old man in pigeon-English. 'Me comee find white hurdee-girlee,' said Walt. 'You see hurdee-girlee?'

The old man said something that sounded like 'Humf!' and then began to speak rapidly in Chinese.

I turned and quickly scanned the Dope Fiends in their bunks. Belle was in the dimmest corner on the lowest bunk. I slipped off my wooden-soled sandals & left them beside some others inside the door & padded silently across the beaten earth floor.

Belle's eyes were half closed. When I whispered her name in her ear she did not respond. She was wearing her red and pink dress but without the hoops. She must have taken them off and left them at her crib. Her hat and parasol, too. But the little beaded purse still hung around her wrist.

I could hear the old Chinaman still demanding

something of Walt – money probably – so with my back still to them, I slipped my seven-shooter into the pocket of my loose pants. Then I reached forward & quietly undid the snap of her purse & and felt inside.

Success!

My piece of paper was there! There was also some paper money by the feel of it, as well as her small powder flask and lead balls, but my gold coin was gone. With pounding heart and dry mouth, I slipped the Letter and a few dollar bills into my pocket along with the Smith & Wesson's seven-shooter. I left some money in her purse, along with the powder flask and balls, so as not to arouse suspicion.

As I started to move away, Belle slowly turned her head and I saw her half-closed eyes try to focus as she looked at me. She opened her mouth to say something but I pressed my finger against her lips. Then I moved over to the bunk next to hers and pretended to busy myself with the objects laid out on a low table.

There was a little alcohol lamp there that burned with a blue flame & a wooden box full of something that looked like brown putty & a long bamboo pipe with a clay bowl at one end.

I heard the jingle of spurs as Walt and Boz came over to Belle's bunk. From beneath the rim of my straw hat I watched Walt search her. She was so sleepy that she hardly protested.

'There,' said Walt at last, tossing Boz the Double Deringer. 'You can keep that as a souvenir.'

Boz took it with his left hand and put it inside his vest. I saw that his right hand was bandaged.

Walt stood up and cursed. 'That danged kid was lying. She don't have that Letter. Let's go.'

'But she was the Hurdy what shot me,' whined Boz. 'I'm gonna pay her back.'

With his left hand he pulled his Colt's Navy Revolver from his pocket and pressed the end of the barrel against her forehead.

Belle had betrayed me & tied me up & robbed me, but I did not want to see her murdered.

With my right hand still in my pocket I cocked the hammer of my Smith & Wesson's seven-shooter. It might not be accurate, but from only two feet away I could not miss.

Despite the promise to my dying ma, I was prepared to use it to save Belle's life.

I said to myself, 'If Boz cocks his piece I will shoot him.'

Thankfully I did not have to.

Before he could pull back the hammer, Walt put a hand on his arm. 'Not now, Boz,' he said in a low growl. 'And not here. But I promise you will get your revenge later.'

'Yeah,' said Boz. 'A bullet in the brain is too good for her. I'm gonna make her suffer. Let's get out of here. Let's find that kid.'

They exited the Opium Den and I nearly fainted from relief & also from the smell of the pipe smoke which was making me light-headed.

I tried to think what to do.

I had got my Letter back and I needed somewhere safe to stay until I could take it to the Recorder's Office the next morning.

I also thought I should warn Belle that her life was in

danger from a vengeful Boz. Yes, she had betrayed me, but I did not want to see her suffer.

It seemed to me the best place to spend the night would be right where I was. Walt and his pards would not come back here anytime soon. There were a few empty bunks up high and I could sleep on one of those.

I went over to the Chinaman and when I lifted my head to look at him he opened his eyes wide in Expression No. 4: Surprise. I guess he could now see I was not a Chinese boy.

I took out a $1 bill and said, 'How much to spend the night?'

His eyes narrowed again. '$5 for pipe and bunk,' he said.

I said, 'I do not want a pipe. Just a place to spend the night.'

He said, 'Does this look like boarding house? You pay $5. You get pipe and bunk for two-three hours. Then go.'

'Please?' I said. I pulled out the other two bills. 'I can pay you $3. Just a little bunk up high? Just until that lady goes? No pipe.'

The old Celestial pursed his lips.

'Please?' I said again. 'It is all I have.' Then I added. 'I'm a friend of Ping's.'

'Ping?' he said. 'Which Ping?'

'Ping the nephew of Hong Wo,' I said.

Once again the old man's eyes opened wide.

He glanced around and then scowled up at me.

'All right. $1 for bunk no pipe. You go up there.'

'If I fall asleep will you wake me up when that lady goes?'

He gave a short nod. 'I will wake you.'

I gave him the $1 and went over to the bunks across the smoky cave from Belle and climbed up to the topmost bunk, which was vacant. I took off my straw-plate hat and rested my head on it. There was only a greasy rush mat on the hard wood but I soon felt a delicious warmth in my bare toes. The sensation crept up my feet and legs and body. By and by I felt warm all over, like I was floating in a tub of hot water. My twisted ankle stopped throbbing and all my bruises stopped hurting. Best of all, I felt my grief seep away and a strange calm replace it.

I must have fallen asleep because I had a beautiful dream. I saw Ma Evangeline and Pa Emmet. They were walking hand in hand along the Streets of Glory. Heaven looked kind of like Virginia City, only flat, not steep & with buildings made of jewels instead of raw planks & streets made of gold as pure as glass. There were trees there, too. They had heavy green leaves and big waxy flowers that glowed red and yellow and blue. The flowers gave off the sweetest perfume I have ever smelled.

Once in Salt Lake City I saw a hot air balloon rise up into the blue sky. My heart felt like that balloon. I felt I could float up into the air and be carried along by a joyful breeze.

Then someone was shaking me and I felt a series of stinging slaps on my cheeks.

I opened my eyes and saw a face swim into view: the wrinkled and sallow face of an old man.

He seemed to be the wisest man who ever lived and I gazed at him happily.

'Chop, chop!' he said with a scowl. 'Your lady friend going, so you must go, too!'

Sitting up, I banged my head on the low rock roof of the cave. This reminded me to put my straw plate hat on again. The cold earth floor reminded me to put on my wooden-soled sandals waiting for me at the door. I emerged into the frosty night. The snow had stopped & the sky had cleared & a million stars blazed overhead.

My head was throbbing & I felt groggy & stupid. However, a few deep breaths of the icy air brought me to my senses just in time to see Belle disappear into one of the dark alleys of Chinatown. I hurried after her. By the time I caught up I still had a headache but at least I felt more alert.

'Belle!' I said, tugging her sleeve. 'Belle, stop!'

She turned and looked at me, a frown creasing her smooth forehead. Her hair was half undone and wisps fell down around her bare shoulders. The fog around us had lifted and the dim lights of a few hanging paper lanterns showed me that her pretty pink and red dress was ripped at the bodice.

'Who are you?' she said. 'What do you want?'

'It's me: P.K.'

She stared at me. 'P.K.?'

I nodded. 'I am in disguise like a Detective. You can't go back to your crib, Belle. Walt and his men are after me now, and they might look for me there. They are real mad at you and if they find you they will carve you up alive.'

She looked at me & then her lower lip quivered & she began to cry. 'Oh, P.K.!' she said. 'I am scared. I had a dream they came when I was down at Ah Sing's.'

'They did come,' I said. 'And Boz was about to blow your brains out.'

'They tore my best dress,' said Belle. 'And they robbed me. And you say I can't go home? What will I do!'

'I know a safe place,' I said. 'You can come with me. Then tomorrow you can get the first stagecoach out of town.'

'Yes,' she said. 'Oh, P.K. I am sorry I tied you up and robbed you. It's just that I love to smoke a pipe. It is the only thing that brings me joy in this godforsaken place.'

We climbed up steep and snowy Taylor Street, keeping alert for shadows that might be Walt and his pards. My head still throbbed & I was also dizzy & a little sick from the Opium Smoke or the thin air or both. Once I slipped but Belle helped me up. We were both trembling with cold by the time we reached B Street. It was still lively and busy up there, even though it was probably 2 or 3 oclock in the morning. The busy boardwalk made me feel safe but I did not breathe a sigh of relief until we stood outside the front door of Isaiah Coffin's Ambrotype & Photographic Gallery. I fished in my medicine pouch & pulled out the key with frozen fingers & the door opened with a welcome tinkle of the bell.

It was dark in there but not too cold and there was enough light from the street torches for us to see. I showed Belle the buffalo skin draped over the couch which I had been dreaming of. She lay down on the couch & wrapped the buffalo skin around her & closed her eyes.

I was tired, too, but I knew I had to take my Letter to the Recorder's Office first thing the next morning. I did not think they would let me in if I was dressed as a Celestial.

And what if Walt remembered seeing a young Chinese boy in the restaurant & in the Opium Den, and put two and two together? Also, my pants were damp & cold from where I had slipped in the snow and fallen down.

Tired as I was, I found some matches and lit a lamp and went back into the costume closet next door.

I took off my damp Celestial outfit & wooden clogs & I chose the smartest suit of clothes I could find. Striped serge pantaloons, a starched white linen shirt, a red velvet waistcoat & a blue jacket with brass buttons. I had to roll up the cuffs of the pants and the sleeves of the shirt, but the jacket fit all right. I found an old plug hat & shiny black brogans. They were all too big, but I used folded newspaper to line the hat and three pairs of woolen socks to make the shoes fit more snugly.

As I sat on the chair to lace them up, I thought of my school shoes & that made me think of ma & pa lying in a pool of blood among the scattered flour on the bare floorboards of our little log cabin down in Temperance. I felt a wave of dizziness & my heart was racing so I sat & took a few deep breaths until it passed.

Then I stood & looked at myself in the mirror.

I tried to view myself as a stranger might.

The lamplit reflection showed a boy with short black hair, a muddy complexion & slightly slanting black eyes. My face betrayed no expression. I tried smiling but it looked strange & felt even stranger.

I found a comb & some hair oil & slicked my short hair back from my forehead. Now I looked like the son of a prosperous banker or stockbroker. Spanish maybe. Or Italian. Even Cornish. Some of the Cornish miners in Dayton have real dark hair & eyes.

'Rather,' I said, in an English accent. I am good at doing an English accent because my foster ma came from England & I had lived with her for two years.

I checked that my Letter was in my medicine pouch and I discovered I still had the folded WANTED poster of Walt and two dollar bills in there as well. I tried putting my Smith & Wesson's seven-shooter in the right-hand pocket of my trowsers. It fit nicely. I had promised Ma Evangeline I would not kill anyone but it felt good to have it there all the same.

There were no blankets back there but I found the heavy woolen overcoat of a Union officer and I wrapped that around myself.

I blew out the lamp and went back into the gallery to make sure Belle was still there.

She was fast asleep and snoring softly. Lying there wrapped in a buffalo skin before the dimly lit scene of the Great Plains, she reminded me a little of my Indian ma.

I lay down behind the couch on a Brussels carpet & took out my Smith & Wesson's seven-shooter & checked the cylinder & put it on the floor beside me.

The floor beneath the carpet was hard & cold and I doubted I would get much sleep, but when I closed my eyes I went out like a candle in a gale.

LEDGER SHEET 27

THE NEXT MORNING I WOKE TO THE SOUND OF A tinkling bell & the smell of fresh coffee.

I opened my eyes.

I was in a room with a partly glass roof that showed blue sky.

For a moment I could not think where I was.

Then it all came flooding back.

I had spent half the night in an Opium Den down in Chinatown and now I was protecting a Soiled Dove named Belle from desperados who wanted to torture and kill us both.

I heard the door close and from underneath the couch I could see a pair of shiny black shoes and the cuffs of a pair of gray trowsers.

Then a man's voice exclaimed, 'Sacray blur! Who are you?'

'Oh, hello, sir,' came Belle's sleepy voice. I heard the

couch above me creak. 'My name is Belle Donne. Who are you?'

'I am Isaiah Coffin, the owner of this establishment. I demand to know what you are doing on my couch.' He had an accent like Ma Evangeline's and I deduced from this that he was English.

Belle said, 'I am sheltering here from three desperados who want to kill me. P.K.?' she said. 'Are you here?'

'Yes, ma'am,' I said, and stood up.

'Zounds!' said Isaiah Coffin, as he saw me rising up from behind the couch. 'What is going on here?'

Brilliant sunlight from the east-facing window illuminated the man standing in the open doorway. Isaiah Coffin wore a black stovepipe hat & a blue frock coat & a red cravat. He had symmetrical features. His hair was light brown & his eyes were gray. He had a feathery blond mustache & billy goat beard. In one hand he held a key & in the other a pot of coffee. He also had a folded newspaper under one arm.

'I am a friend of Ping's,' I said. 'He gave me a key to your shop.'

'Ping!' said the man, putting down the coffee-pot and paper and replacing the key in his vest pocket. 'When I get my hands on him! '

'I am sorry!' cried Ping, squeezing past Isaiah Coffin and into the room. 'I am sorry! I told him not to touch anything.' Ping's eyes opened wide when he saw Belle. Then he narrowed them again & looked at me & mouthed something I could not understand.

Isaiah Coffin ignored Ping and removed his stovepipe hat and placed it on the hat rack. Then he frowned. 'Is that one of my costumes?' he said to me. Then he looked at Belle. 'And is that my buffalo skin?'

'Yes, sir,' she replied. 'I am sorry.' She shrugged it off to reveal her torn dress.

Isaiah Coffin's eyes grew wide when he saw her state of disarray. So did Ping's.

'Sacray blur!' said Isaiah Coffin, shielding his eyes as if from the blazing sun. 'Please cover yourself, Madame.'

'But I have nothing else to wear.'

Isaiah Coffin gestured towards the costume closet. 'Find yourself something in there,' he said. 'But leave that dress of yours as collateral. And you!' Here he turned to address me. 'You say you are a friend of Ping's?'

'He's not my friend,' said Ping. 'But he will soon be rich. He will pay me five hundred dollar cash and he will pay you for wearing clothes.' Ping looked at me. 'Won't you?'

'Yes, sir,' I said, putting the plug hat on my head. 'Yes, I will. In about an hour or so I will be a millionaire.'

'What did you say your name was?' asked Isaiah Coffin. He had a way of standing, very straight but with his shoulders slightly back.

'My name is P.K. Pinkerton,' I said in an English accent like his.

'P.K. Pinkerton,' he said. 'Unusual name.'

'Isaiah Coffin,' I said. 'Unusual name.'

'Tooshay,' he said. His eyes had a kind of twinkle in them.

I said, 'Beg pardon?'

He said, 'Tooshay is French for "you got me there".'

He took a mug from a shelf near the hat rack and poured himself a cup of black coffee.

I said, 'I am partial to coffee, too. Black, no sugar.'

'Are you indeed?'

He found a china teacup from a decorative tea set on a table & poured me a cup.

'Ping?' said Isaiah Coffin. 'Would you like some coffee, too?'

'No, boss,' said Ping. 'I like tea.' He was still scowling at me.

'I like coffee,' came a female voice from the clothes cupboard. 'Cream and three sugars.'

'Ping,' said Isaiah Coffin. 'Go fill this jug with cream from the Colombo Restaurant.' He handed Ping a small jug decorated with rosebuds.

Ping shot me a final scowl and left the shop.

I sat on Isaiah Coffin's couch. It was still faintly warm from Belle's body. I blew on the surface of my coffee and took a sip. I remembered to lift my little finger as Ma Evangeline had taught me. I was beginning to realize that wearing different clothes made me feel different. This get-up made me feel high-tone and confident.

'Make yourself at home,' said Isaiah Coffin, raising one eyebrow.

'Thank you,' I replied.

He rolled his eyes and came to sit next to me. 'Tell

me,' he said. 'Who are these "desperados" after that young woman?'

'Actually, they are after me,' I said. My English accent made me use bigger words. 'They are called Whittlin Walt, Extra Dub and Boz Burton. They killed my foster parents down in Temperance and then scalped them to make it look as if Indians did it.'

His smile vanished & I saw the blood drain from his face.

'Whittlin Walt?' he said.

I said, 'Yes. They call him that because he likes to whittle pieces off his victims while quoting Walt Whitman.' I removed the folded WANTED poster from my medicine pouch & handed it to him.

He opened it and his gray eyes widened.

'D-mn me!' said Isaiah Coffin & then added, 'Pardon my French.'

I knew he did not really mean pardon his French. He meant pardon him saying a word that would send him straight to that fiery place. I was coming to realize that everybody in Virginia cussed like drunken mule-drivers.

I was putting the folded WANTED poster back in my medicine bag when the door opened with a tinkle and Ping put his head in. 'Colombo Restaurant closed,' he said.

Still using my English accent, I said, 'That is probably because Titus Jepson lost the tip of his pinkie last night and wants to preserve his remaining digits.'

'D-mn me!' said Isaiah Coffin. He forgot to ask me to

pardon his French. To Ping he said, 'Well, go somewhere else then.' To me he said, 'Why is he after you?'

I said, 'I have a document he wants. Mr. Dan De Quille of the Territorial Enterprise said it was the Holy Grail of the Comstock and that it could make The Bearer a millionaire.'

He took a sip of coffee & stared into his cup. 'P.K., old chap, you should be careful whom you trust. Don't go around telling everybody you have a valuable letter that could make the bearer a millionaire.'

'That is good advice,' I said, also taking a sip of coffee. 'I can never tell whom to trust and whom not to trust.'

'May I give you some more good advice?' said Isaiah Coffin. 'In this town, don't trust anybody. There's only one reason people come to Virginia, and that is Mammon. Everyone who comes here wants gold or silver or money of some sort.'

'Even you?' I said.

'Even me.' He finished his coffee & put the cup on the floor. 'I might suggest that you could trust Mr. S. B. Rooney – the pastor here in Virginia – but I have never darkened the door of his church so I cannot be sure.'

I saw his eyes widen as he looked over my shoulder. It was Expression No. 4: Surprise.

I turned to see that Belle Donne had reappeared from the clothing cupboard. She was wearing a starched white bonnet and a black dress that buttoned all the way up to her chin. She was warming her hands in a fur muff.

'Why you are quite transformed, Miss Donne,' said Isaiah Coffin, rising to his feet. 'You look just like a school marm.'

'I know,' said Belle. 'Hideous, ain't it?'

'Not at all,' said Isaiah Coffin. 'I find it quite charming.'

'P.K.,' said Belle. 'Did I hear you say you had recovered that Letter?'

'Yes,' I said. 'And I intend to take it to the Recorder's Office up on A Street right now.'

She said, 'I am afraid that is not going to happen.'

She let her muff drop to the ground and lifted a Colt's Baby Dragoon and pointed it at us.

'Hands up,' said Belle. 'Both of you. Give me that Letter, P.K. And no funny business.'

I thought, 'That Belle has tricked me once again.'

I also thought, 'I cannot even tell when someone is about to draw down on me.'

And finally, 'How can I ever be a Detective?'

LEDGER SHEET 28

MY THORN HAD BETRAYED ME, BUT MY GIFT – MY keen observational skills – might save me yet.

Belle Donne was aiming a cocked Colt's Baby Dragoon Revolver at my chest. It had an ivory grip. I recognized it from the clothing cupboard.

'Give me that Letter,' she said. 'Then no harm will come to you.'

'That is unfair,' I said. 'I risked my life to save you.'

'It is true,' said Belle, 'that you have been kind to me. I do not want to shoot you. But I will if I have to. Now give me that Letter.'

'Very well,' I said.

I stood up.

'What are you doing?' she said.

I told a lie. 'The Letter is in my pocket,' I said. I put my hand in my pocket and pulled out my Smith & Wesson's seven-shooter & drew down on her.

She quickly aimed her Colt at my leg and pulled the trigger. Nothing happened.

'What the hell?' she said.

I cocked my piece. 'I recognized that Colt from the clothing cupboard,' I said. 'It is unloaded and busted. Now get *your* hands up.'

'You will not shoot me,' she said with Expression No. 3: Disgust.

I fired into the ceiling, just missing the sky-window. My shot brought down a satisfying shower of dust & plaster. I cocked my gun again.

Belle cursed in language unfit for publication but she lifted her hands.

Isaiah Coffin chuckled and started to lower his.

'Both of you,' I said. 'Keep your hands up.' I pointed my gun at Belle. 'You,' I said. 'Sit on the couch with your back to him.'

'D-mn you,' said Belle. But she did as I asked.

'Mr. Coffin,' I said. 'Would you please remove your cravat and bind her hands behind her?'

'Which is it to be?' Isaiah Coffin asked me. 'Do you want me to keep my hands up or bind her hands?'

'Bind her hands. I am going to tie you up to her.'

Isaiah Coffin removed his cravat and began to bind Belle's wrists.

'I do not understand why you are doing this to me,' he said.

'You told me not to trust anybody,' said I. 'And I think that is good advice.'

'Tooshay,' he said and then 'Vwa la!' as he finished tying her wrists. 'Now what?'

'Take off your shoes,' I said, 'and pull out the laces.'

Isaiah Coffin bent over and began to take off his shoes.

'Untie me, P.K.,' said Belle. 'And I will split the proceeds with you fifty-fifty.'

'I already have a partner,' I said. 'And he will be back any minute with the cream. Mr. Coffin, would you please slide your shoes over to me? And use one of the laces to tie your ankles together.'

Isaiah Coffin sighed deeply but did as I asked.

The next bit was tricky. I had to tie his wrists with my right hand while keeping my revolver trained on them with my left. But I managed to do it. Then I tied Isaiah Coffin's wrists to Belle's.

They were now sitting back to back, perched on the edge of the couch with their wrists tied tightly in as many knots as I could manage.

'Now close your eyes, both of you,' I said, 'and count to one hundred aloud.'

As the two of them started to count out loud, I went to the front door and flipped the sign inside the window of the door so that it read CLOSED. Then I went out & locked it from the outside. I peeped back through the window to make sure their eyes were still closed.

Belle had opened one eye but quickly closed it again when she saw me looking in.

I released the hammer of my seven-shooter & slipped it into my pocket. Then I patted the medicine bag which

145

I had tucked safely under my shirt & jacket. I felt the Letter crinkle reassuringly.

As I turned to go towards the Recorder's Office, I saw Ping coming towards me along the boardwalk. He had a brimming jug of cream in his hand and was concentrating on not spilling any. I did not want to go into long explanations about why I had tied up his boss, so before he could look up and spot me I quickly went into the tobacconist's shop next door to wait for him to pass by.

Bloomfield's Tobacco Emporium was a narrow shop – more like a long corridor – but there were shelves on the wall & every inch was taken up with colored tins & pouches of tobacco. There were pipes & cigars, too. And there was a 6 ft tall painted wooden Indian standing just inside the front door.

It smelled like Pa Emmet in there & for a moment my vision grew blurry. Then I blinked & it cleared.

'Hello,' said a girl's voice. 'May I help you?'

I turned to see the girl from the other day coming towards me.

'I am just browsing,' I said.

'You remind me of my cousin Moshee.' She held out her hand. 'My name is Becky Bloomfield,' she said. 'What's yours?'

I shook her moist, warm hand.

'My name is P.K.,' I said.

She had pale skin & the longest eyelashes I had ever seen. Without letting go of my hand, she said, 'This is my father's shop. His name is Solomon but everyone calls him Smiley. My friends call me Bee because I am sweet as honey. We are moving everything down to our C Street shop soon. Until we sell this place he lets me watch it after school and on the weekends. Do you go to school? I am at the First Ward School with Miss Feather.'

I removed my hand from her grip & said, 'I go to school down in Dayton.'

'Do you live in Dayton?' she said, fluttering her eyelashes.

She was standing too close for my liking, so I took a step back.

She took a step closer. 'How old are you?' she said. 'I am eleven but everyone says I am tall for my age.'

'I am twelve,' I said, taking another step back. I felt something bumpy pressing into my shoulder blades & realized she had me backed up against the wooden Indian.

Bee Bloomfield took a step closer. I could smell minty sozodont tooth powder on her breath. It was what Ma Evangeline used on special occasions to make her teeth white. Bee Bloomfield said, 'Would you kiss me, P.K.?'

I said, 'Beg pardon?'

She said, 'Adelicia says she has been kissed & she's younger than I am. So have Hannah & Susan. I'm the only girl in my classroom who's never kissed a boy.'

She had closed her eyes & was aiming her puckered lips right at me.

I said, 'I do not like to be touched. Goodbye!'

I writhed out from under her just in time. She kissed that wooden statue, I bet.

I hurried out of the Tobacco Shop & pulled my plug hat down lower & turned right & crossed muddy Taylor Street, heading in the direction of the Recorder's Office.

I thought, 'What is it about Virginia City? The people here either want to kill you or kiss you.'

LEDGER SHEET 29

IN SPITE OF THE PREVIOUS NIGHT'S SNOW, IT WAS almost warm. The early morning sun was painting long blue shadows of the town up the slope of Mount Davidson. It was the strangest weather I had ever experienced. Yesterday it had been hot. Last night it snowed. Now it was clear again & the warm sun was melting the snow. There was just a light dusting of it where the road was still in shadow. The middle of the thoroughfare had already been churned into mud by the never-ending procession of Buggies & Quartz Wagons.

The bright clear day raised my spirits. For once I was not being pursued by desperados with blazing guns. I had my priceless Document & within the hour – God willing – I would be on a stage to Chicago.

I crossed over the muddy thoroughfare to the west side of B Street & my heavy brogans made the boardwalk echo as I continued north. I gave the brown dog outside Fulton's

Meat Market a wide berth & crossed Union Street without mishap. Across the street I could see the back entrance of the International Hotel & the 40 foot flag-staff rising up from its roof. When I reached Sutton I turned left up it.

There was no boardwalk there & the melting snow was making it a river. When I was halfway up that short side street, a horse coming down started slipping & he got spooked & his driver almost lost control & I almost got trampled.

I hugged the brick wall of an end building and made my way up that slippery slope in Satan's Playground & when I reached A Street, I offered up a prayer of thanks that I was on level ground again. Then I took a moment to catch my breath & make sure I was not being followed & also to get my bearings.

Catty corner across the street was the Territorial Enterprise. And across the street from it was the Recorder's Office. I could see the sign hanging down.

I was waiting to cross over when I saw a tall man loitering on the corner opposite. He had a black slouch hat & a biscuit-colored linen duster coat & the biggest Adam's Apple I have ever seen. It was Extra Dub.

My whole body suddenly went cold & my heart speeded up.

Instead of crossing over Sutton, I crossed over A Street to the west side. From this vantage point, I could see another suspicious character about fifty feet up my side of the street. He was leaning on a wooden pillar directly opposite the Recorder's Office. He also wore a black hat and beige duster. When he turned to spit, I saw that he had a broken nose and two black eyes, one of them a little squintier than the other. It was Boz. I looked down real quick so he wouldn't catch my eye.

I took a deep breath, and with my head still down I walked towards him, crossing the muddy street at a break in traffic. I stepped up onto the boardwalk and gave the PONY EXPRESS door of the Territorial Enterprise a businesslike knock. Without waiting for an answer I swiftly turned the handle, praying that the door would be open.

Thankfully it was & I got safely inside.

I was surprised to find the newspaper office deserted and the Washington Printing Press silent.

I went over to the window and peeped out.

If I looked left I could just see Boz, leaning against his column. If I looked right I could see Extra Dub patrolling the opposite corner. Then I turned to study the Recorder's Office across the street. There was a steady stream of people & carts and also some horses hitched to the post outside that blocked my view of the front door. But then a man unhitched one of the horses & swung up into the saddle & rode off. That was when I spotted Walt. He was sitting on a bench right outside the Recorder's Office with his legs stuck out & a black slouch hat pulled down over his eyes, just as if he was sleeping. But underneath his hat I could just see his jaw working now and then on a chaw of tobacco.

He was not sleeping. He was on the lookout for me. And he was not moving any time soon.

LEDGER SHEET 30

I STOOD AT THE WINDOW OF THE TERRITORIAL Enterprise Newspaper and peeped out. Yes, there was no doubt about it: Walt and his pards had staked out a claim on that Recorder's Office and they were waiting for me.

I thought about what I should do next.

I might be able to pass by them in my rich boy's garb.

But what if Walt had finally guessed that I was partial to disguises? What if he had given his men orders to stop anyone under five feet tall? Even with my brogans and plug hat I was under five feet.

'May I help you?' said a voice behind me.

I turned to see a strangely attired man coming in from a back door. He was doing up his pants and I deduced he had been to the privy.

He was clean-shaven with short reddish-brown hair & jutting eyebrows & some whiskers at the side of his ears. His pants were too big & his flannel shirt was too small. I could smell soap & starch.

'We are closed today,' he drawled.

I said, 'I am looking for Mr. Dan De Quille.'

'Dan is not here.' The man pulled a pipe out of his pocket & stuck it in his mouth. It was not lit but it still stank & I instantly recognized the smell: half tobacco & half the remains of some dead critter.

I said, 'Mr. Sam Clemens? Is that you?'

He took a few steps forward & peered into my face. 'P.K. Pinkerton?' he said. 'Is that you?'

I nodded.

He chuckled & said, 'I did not recognize you. What is your transformation in aid of?'

'New disguise,' I said. 'Whittlin Walt saw me last night and now he thinks I am a little girl who likes pink. So I cannot use that get-up again.'

'That is too bad. You made a rather fetching little girl. As for me, I have been shaved and shorn, bathed and deloused. I am wearing a new suit of clothes, courtesy of Mr. Bach down at Selfridge & Bach's Bathhouse. Do you like my whiskers?' he lifted his chin and turned to show me his profile. 'Bach tells me they are just like those of General Burnside and that they are the Latest Fashion.'

'Where is Dan?' I asked, looking around. 'And all the other reporters? Don't you have a newspaper to get out?'

'This morning's issue has already been delivered by an army of small boys,' he said. 'And we don't publish on Sunday, so this is our day off. Everybody is either at home or still down at the Old Corner Saloon. By the way, you are now famous.' He used his pipe to tap a newspaper lying open on the big table.

I stepped forward and looked where he was pointing. I saw a small column on page three.

There was a caption saying:

TRAGIC DOUBLE MURDER IN TEMPERANCE

And beneath it as follows:

Reports of the death of the Reverend Emmet Jones and his wife Evangeline of Temperance near Como reached us yesterday evening. Certain witnesses say the couple were murdered by some of the local Paiute Indians, but this claim has not yet been confirmed, so retaliation would be unwise. Do not panic! The couple's twelve-year-old adopted son went missing about the same time as the murder. He answers to the name of P.K. or "Pinky" Pinkerton and he is the prime suspect. It is believed he stole a document of great value from the kind-hearted folk who took him in and nurtured him. The boy is not quite five feet tall, with short black hair, dark brown eyes and a sallow complexion owing to his being half Indian. If you should see him, please turn him in at the Marshal's office as he is wanted for questioning. Caution recommended, he could be armed and dangerous.

'Who wrote this?' I said.

'Dan De Quille.'

'He makes it sound like I robbed and murdered my foster parents. He does not even mention Whittlin Walt and his pards.'

'This article is designed to appease Walt and his pards, not aggravate them. Dan stopped by the saloon last night to tell us what happened.' Sam Clemens struck a match and tried to light his foul-smelling pipe. 'He was in a terrible state. He thinks Walt will whittle him for pretending you were his daughter. Dan was planning to catch the early stage to Carson City.'

I said, 'I am sorry he is a fugitive on account of me but that does not give him the right to tell such a story or to ask people to turn me in.'

'He only wrote that about turning you in because he thinks you would be safest in jail. He told the Marshal what really happened. You must not be too hard on old Dan.'

Sam finally got his pipe going & said between puffs, 'He also said to tell you he was wrong in advising you to take your Letter to the Recorder's Office. He said you should take it to the Notary Public first.'

'What is a Notary Public?' I said.

'It is a man who will stamp your documents to certify them and make them legal.'

I went back to the window and looked out at Walt and his pards. They seemed to be settled in for the day.

I said, 'Do you mean to say I do not have to go to that Recorder's Office across the street? I could register this Letter as mine with the Notary Public?'

Sam Clemens shrugged. 'I do not really understand such things,' he said. 'But, yes: I believe that is what Dan meant.'

Just when all seemed darkest, a spark of hope was kindled in my heart.

I turned and pointed to the back door. 'Can you get out through that door, or does it only lead to the privy?'

'If you don't mind picking your way around the rubbish pile and Old Joe's chicken run you can get out that way,' he said.

'Do you know where the Notary Public is?' I asked.

He shook his head. 'I don't,' he said. 'But there is a *Directory to Virginia City* right there. It will tell you where to go.' He went over to a desk & flipped open a book & a few moments later he said, 'Here it is: W. Hutchins, Notary Public for Storey County, Nevada Territory, B Street opposite the Virginia City Hotel. And according to this,' here he flipped over some more pages, 'the Virginia City Hotel is on the southwest corner of B and Sutton. I guess it is not far from the International

Hotel.' He closed the book. 'Just a hop, skip and a jump. Come over here, P.K.,' he said. 'Have a look at this.'

He pointed to the framed Panoramic View of Virginia City.

It had been dim last night but now I could see it better. It showed Virginia City as a bird flying up from the south might view it. The mountain's peak was on the left and it sort of slanted down to the lower right, with five or six streets descending this slope like steps. Around this cunning scene, the artist had made a border composed of about 30 buildings. They were seen front on, rather than from a bird's eye view.

'What are those little buildings around the picture?' I said.

'According to Dan, those are some Virginia City landmarks. There we are, right there.'

I stood in admiration. One of the buildings was the Territorial Enterprise. It showed the sign and the two flags and the door with PONY EXPRESS EXTRA painted on it. There was even a boy about my age selling a newspaper to a gentleman in a stovepipe hat.

'Look,' I said. 'There is the brown dog outside Fulton's Meat Market. And there is a hardware store with a stove and coffee-pots on the roof.'

'And there is my favorite landmark,' said Sam Clemens. 'Piper's Old Corner Saloon. Cunning picture, ain't it?'

'Yes,' I said, and brought my nose right up to admire it.

A notice at the bottom read: *Virginia City, Nevada Territory, 1861. Published by Grafton T. Brown.*

Although the town had grown a lot in the past year, I recognized many buildings as unchanged. I saw the spire of the church on D Street, the corrals of the livery stables & the smokestacks of mine buildings. It showed how the streets were laid out on the side of Mount Davidson. I could clearly see Streets A through D and some mine buildings scattered about, too.

'Your Notary Public will be right about here,' said Sam Clemens, tapping the glass above B Street with his pipe-stem.

I said, 'Maybe I can go around this way.' I marked out a possible route with my finger.

'Why not just go straight down Sutton and turn right?' he said.

I went over to the window and looked out. 'First of all, because it is a slippery river of mud. Second of all, because Walt and his pards are waiting for me across the street,' I said.

He came and looked over my shoulder. 'Dang my buttons,' he said. 'So they are. Perhaps I will go out the back way, too. I was planning to waltz on down to C Street, in search of a decent suit of clothes. Clothes make the man, you know. Naked people have little or no influence on society.'

I nodded absently. I was considering the best route to take.

Sam Clemens went over to the hat rack. There were two slouch hats there. For a moment his hand hovered over an old one covered in pale yellow dust. Then he chose the other one. It was newer-looking, and coffee-colored. He put it on his head and went to the back door. When he reached it, he turned & said to me, 'Would you like me to accompany you as far as the Notary Public?'

I was about to say Yes but then I remembered the lesson Virginia City was teaching me: Don't trust anybody.

'No thank you,' I said. 'I will go alone.'

'Suit yourself,' he said. 'I wish you good luck. I hope to recognize you next time we meet, but if I don't it ain't rudeness, it's just stupidity.'

'Likewise,' I said.

He grinned & tipped his slouch hat & went out.

I waited for a while and then went to the back door, too.

I opened it a crack and peeked out.

I could see the outhouse & the chicken run & a place where they burned rubbish & the mountainside sloping up.

I went out into the bright morning and looked cautiously around. There was nobody there but some chickens.

Somewhere up on the mountainside I heard a quail say, 'Chicago! Chicago!'

I thought, 'I'll be on my way soon.'

I picked my way through the waste area and sage bushes, going up the mountain.

I soon reached the street above A Street. It was not so much a street as a muddy track. From here I could see a large white building with a big smokestack and a sign that read MEXICAN MINE. Turning to look down over the town, I could see my best route was to go north a block, then down Carson to B Street and then to double back.

I took a deep breath of the thin air & lifted my eyes & gazed out at the 100 mile view. The sun was warm & the air was perfumed with sage & I could feel the comforting thump of the mountain.

I thought, 'I am always happiest when I am on my own.'

Then I thought, 'Does that make me a Heartless Misfit?'

I took one more breath & then started towards Carson Street up ahead.

A faint crash made me look around.

Down below me, a mine car had dumped a load of dirt & rocks & other trash. Somewhere down in the bowels of the mountain, men were digging like ants. The car seemed to be hanging in space over a cliff but as the dust cleared I could see it had gone to the end of a track propped up by trellis supports, like half a bridge. Now a miner was pulling it back the way it had come. I noticed the tracks led back up to an opening in the mountainside.

'See how man has scarred the mountainside in his quest for wealth?' said a voice behind me. I turned to see a Negro sitting on a collapsible camp-chair. He was sketching. A jagged & upthrusting boulder had hidden him from view until now.

'Holes and pits and dumps,' said the black man. 'Some people think it doesn't matter. They think this part of the world is ugly anyway.' He gestured around him with his pencil. 'But I think this barren mountain is strangely beautiful.'

'I like the desert,' I said. 'I like it a lot.'

'I like it, too,' he said.

I had never seen a Negro up close to talk to. His cheeks were smooth & I reckoned he was not much more than twenty.

'Are you a runaway Slave?' I said.

He laughed. 'No,' he said. 'I am freeborn. Born in Philadelphia.'

I came closer to him & saw he was making a neat sketch of Virginia City. His style of drawing looked familiar. I looked back up at him. 'Are you Grafton T. Brown?' I said.

His eyes opened wide in Expression No. 4: Surprise.

'Why yes, I am,' he said. 'Have we met?'

I said, 'We have never met but I just saw your Panoramic View of Virginia City in the office of the Territorial Enterprise Newspaper. I think it is the best drawing I have ever seen in my life.'

He showed even white teeth in a No. 1 Genuine Smile.

'And you remembered my name?'

'I'm good at remembering names,' I said. 'But not faces.'

He nodded & put down his pencil. 'I have the same problem, believe it or not. But I have a trick,' he said. 'A trick of telling people apart.'

'I would like to know that Trick,' I said.

'My trick is ears.'

'Ears?' I said.

Grafton T. Brown nodded. 'If you can't tell one person from another, just look at their ears. A person's ear is very distinctive.'

I said, 'That is easy for you to say. You are an artist.'

'Anyone can do it,' he said. 'It is just a matter of training yourself to look. You for example, have quite a delicate ear. It has a flat, squarish earlobe & a smooth upper whorl. The lobe is the part ladies pierce for earrings,' he added, 'and the whorl is the swirly bit around the ear hole. Do you see anything distinctive about my ears?'

I examined his left ear & said, 'Your ears are quite round and small for your head. And your lobe is also rounded.'

'Good.' He pinched his own earlobe between finger & thumb. 'Would you call mine plump, thin or in-between?'

'Plump,' I said. 'But I will not have trouble recognizing you again. You are about the only Negro I have seen here.'

'You would be surprised,' he said, 'at how many of us there are here in Virginia.' He showed his teeth again in a smile. 'White people claim we look alike, but all those bearded miners look the same to me. And I have trouble telling one Celestial from another. Indians are difficult to distinguish, too. That is why it is good to look at people's ears, as well as their faces.'

'Do you live here in Virginia?' I said.

'No,' he said, 'I live in San Francisco. I only come here once or twice a year to clear my head and update my views of this town. You would not believe how much it has grown in just a year.'

I said, 'Have you ever been to Chicago?'

'Once,' he said. 'It was very cold there and that wind is fierce. Is that where you're from?'

'No,' I said. 'But I hope to go there one day.'

'You should come to San Francisco,' he said. 'Now that is a fine city. A lot like this one, in fact, but with the ocean instead of desert. And fine balmy weather.'

In the few moments we had been talking, the wind had got up & had begun to spit grit & flecks of sage-brush in our faces.

'Here comes the Washoe Zephyr,' said Grafton T. Brown. 'That marks the end of my sketching for today.' He put his pencil in his jacket pocket & closed up his drawing pad.

The wind moaned & tugged at our hats.

As we started down the hill I said, 'This wind is real strong. What did you call it?'

He said, 'They call it the Washoe Zephyr. It has been known to fling away roofs and even whole buildings.'

I said, 'Our dictionary at home defines a zephyr as "a warm breeze". This is more like a gale.'

Grafton T. Brown smiled. 'Virginia humor,' he said, hunching his head into his shoulders & putting up his lapels. 'They are a perverse people. They call a hee-hawing mule a Washoe Canary and a gale like this a Zephyr. They don't stop the mining for church on Sunday but they'll be stopping it for the funeral of that poor murdered Hurdy Girl.'

'Hurdy Girl?' I said. I stopped walking and so did he.

163

'A Hurdy Girl,' said Grafton T. Brown, 'is what they call one of those girls who lives down on D Street. A Soiled Dove.'

For a terrible moment I thought he meant Belle. But I had left her tied up to Isaiah Coffin and locked in his studio less than an hour ago.

'What was the name of the murdered Hurdy Girl?' I said.

'Her name was Sally Sampson. People call her Short Sally. Got her throat cut from ear to ear.'

'Who did it?' I asked. My throat was dry.

'They don't know,' he said.

I felt sick. What if Walt and his pards had mistaken Short Sally for Belle? They were cold-hearted Killers who would stop at nothing.

The wind buffeted my back, as if urging me back towards town.

What was I doing loitering on the slopes of Mount Davidson?

I needed to deliver my Letter to the Notary Public as fast as I could.

LEDGER SHEET 32

WITHOUT EVEN BIDDING THE ARTIST GOODBYE, I started running down the mountain.

I soon found myself near the place where they were dumping rubble. I skidded to a stop at the edge of a steep place where the earth fell sharply away. The ground was still damp from the thawing snow & I almost plunged over. Looking down, I saw dirt & chunks of rock & rotten spars of wood all jumbled together. This was not tailings. Tailings were all smooth & pointy, like anthills, because they were made of the fine dust that came out of the Quartz Stamp Mills.

This was a Dump: all bumpy & unstable. This was where that car dumped the rubbish from shafts and tunnels.

I should have gone around it, but I was impatient to get down to the Notary Public on the east side of B Street behind the International Hotel. The howling wind had given me a new sense of urgency. It was like an omen of something bad about to happen.

I leapt down onto the top of the dump and began to descend from boulder to spar. Once or twice I almost fell as a piece of rock shifted beneath my feet or a timber see-sawed. But I did not tumble.

As I reached the bottom, a pale-eyed boy rose up suddenly from a crouching position & put out his hand to check my progress. I was going too fast to stop & so we collided & both fell down. I scrambled to my feet & was going to continue down the mountain. But now I saw two other boys had stood up to block my way & a fourth was coming up behind them.

The first boy was on his feet & his icy blue eyes were narrowed into Expression No. 5: Suspicion.

'What are you doing on our dump?' he said. 'Are you one of the Savage Gang?'

'He ain't no member of the Savage Gang,' said a redheaded boy. He held a splinter of wood about the size of my forearm & was brandishing it like a spear. 'He is one of the tony bunch. Look how he is dressed.'

'Let me by,' I said. Two of the other boys had rocks in their hands. They were no more than ten or eleven but they had a feral look of cornered weasels. I remembered today was Saturday so they were not in school.

They were dressed in old shirts & pants.

I was dressed in a starched white shirt, serge trowsers, waistcoat, jacket & plug hat. And also my sturdy brogans.

Two of them were barefoot.

A fifth boy came down the rubble behind me & grabbed my right arm just above the elbow.

'We can't let you by,' said the first boy. 'We are the Mexican Gang and you are on our territory. You are now our prisoner.'

It was like Olaf & his bully friends all over again.

I did not have time for this today.

I wrenched my right arm free & pulled my seven-shooter out of my pocket & pulled back the hammer & fired it in the air. It did not make a very big bang outdoors & with the wind moaning around us, but it did the trick: they all jumped back. For an instant I smelled gunpowder, then the wind snatched the smoke away. I cocked my pistol again & leveled it at them & swiveled so it pointed at each of them in turn.

Then I said, 'Let me by.'

They let me by.

Once I was safely past them, I released the hammer of my seven-shooter & slipped it back into my pocket & ran. I felt bad that I had aimed a loaded revolver at kids my own age. What would Pa Emmet & Ma Evangeline say? What would my original pa say? But I had a mission. I had to get to the Notary Public.

I glanced back over my shoulder. As I feared, the boys of the Mexican Gang were following me. One of them had got a bow & arrow from somewhere. I pulled out my revolver, but they all jumped back behind a privy. I put away my gun & turned & ran down, dodging between

167

outhouses, sheds and rubbish piles until at last I found myself on A Street.

I was back where I had started.

I did not linger to see whether Walt and his pals were still staking out the Recorder's Office. Instead, I hurriedly crossed the muddy street and found an alley between two buildings. I reckoned it would lead me down to B Street.

I reached a kind of T where the alley went left and right.

I was trying to figure out which way would be the best way to go when a thrumming arrow buried itself in the wooden planks of the building in front of me. That decided me quick. I ran left & then right & emerged onto B Street, near a blacksmith's shop. Across the street was a livery stable and next to it the Fashion Saloon. Over to my right I could see the flag that marked the site of the International Hotel. The Notary Public was between me & it. I was almost there.

I felt that familiar prickly feeling on the back of my neck. I turned & looked behind me. Sure enough, a few members of the Mexican Gang were still in pursuit. When I stuck my hand in my pocket, they all hid behind the back of the smithy.

The sooner I got to the Notary Public, the better.

The wind was howling and making shutters bang.

As I started to cross B to get to the other side, part of a tin roof flew past me, at neck level. A foot to the left and it would have chopped off my head.

It seemed that Virginia City itself was out to get me.

The flying piece of tin caused a pair of horses to rear up and that made a break in the traffic. Taking advantage of it, I dashed across the muddy street. This part of B Street had no boardwalk and I had to do some fancy footwork to avoid horse manure outside the livery stable.

Only a little further, I thought, and I will be safe.

As I began to run, the wind blew some grit in my eyes. That was why I did not see the man in black.

He had just come out of the Fashion Saloon & he was standing outside the swinging doors counting his money when I slammed into him. Some gold coins fell on the muddy ground around us. I heard him curse & felt him clutch at me, but I was up & running again.

However, I did not get far. I ran smack dab into a pair of rock-hard legs clad in gray and yellow checked trowsers. The black-clad torso above the legs was solid as a block of quartz. Worst of all was the face. It was one of the ugliest faces I had ever seen. The man had a big black mustache & bulging eyes that stared in two different directions.

'Let me by,' I said.

'You ain't going nowhere, boy,' he said, and I found myself looking down the twin barrels of a fearsome weapon. 'Make one move and I'll blow your brains out.'

The ugly man held one of those big Le Mats that some Confederate officers favor. It was a combined revolver and shotgun. The top barrel dispensed nine big .40 caliber balls and the bottom barrel had a single load of shot that could take off my entire head.

'Give them back,' said the man with the Le Mat. I could barely hear his deep voice above the moaning of the wind.

'What?' I said. 'Give what back?'

'Those gold coins you stole off Jace.'

'I did not steal any coins,' I said.

'Then where are you going in such a rush?' he said in his bear growl.

'I am going to the Notary Public,' I said. 'It is right behind you, just across the street. Please let me by.'

The man was aiming right between my eyes.

'Are you stupid, boy?' he said.

'No,' I said. 'I am smart.'

'Then why ain't you scared?'

'I *am* scared,' I said. 'I am scared and also angry.'

'You don't look it,' he said.

'That is because I am a Freak of Nature,' I said.

The man's bulging eyes widened & he said, 'Hey, Jace. Lookee here. This boy has a better poker face than you do.'

The man I had jostled appeared beside us. I did not want to turn my head but I could see him out of the corner of my eye. He was tall & slim & dressed all in black, as far as I could see. He was counting his gold coins.

'This here is Poker Face Jace,' said the walleyed man. 'And they call me Stonewall. Maybe you have heard of us.'

'No, sir. I have not heard of you.' I said this without moving.

He pressed the cold barrel of the gun right between my eyes.

170

'If Jace gives the word,' said Stonewall, 'I will blow your brains all over the thoroughfare. Do you believe me?'

'Yes, sir,' I said, 'I believe you.'

Poker Face Jace spoke. 'Ain't you scared?' he asked in a pleasant Southern drawl.

'Yes, sir.'

'You don't look it.'

Poker Face Jace moved round so he could see my face better. As he did so I saw his eyes. They were dark brown and expressionless & I suddenly realized that I had seen him before. He was the gambler who had caught me when I leapt from the gallery of the saloon. At the time I had been wearing a pink calico dress and bonnet. I wondered how long it would take him to recognize me.

'There is no evidence of trepidation about you,' he said. His skin was pale & he had gray hair above his ears, but all the other parts of him were black: his mustache, his eyes, his eyebrows. He was even dressed all in black, from his hat to his boots. The wind whipped his black linen duster against his legs, and then blew it open, giving me a glimpse of the walnut butt of a small pistol in his right-hand pants pocket.

He took a cigar from his coat pocket & examined it. 'Where are you going in such a hurry?' he asked.

'Some kids from the Mexican Gang are after me,' I said. It was not the whole Truth but when I rolled my eyes to the right I could still see a couple of them lurking on the other side of the street. One held an arrow notched and ready, the other clutched a sharp rock in each hand. When they saw

Jace and Stonewall look at them, they turned tail and ran.

'Nasty bullies, indeed,' said Jace. 'And yet your face betrayed no fear then, nor does it now with cold metal pressed against your forehead.' He struck a match on the wall & shielded the flame with his hand & got his cigar going. 'You are right, Stonewall,' he said at last. 'He's got a better poker face than I do. Put up your gun.'

Stonewall uncocked his Le Mat & pointed it up towards the overhang. 'You missing any coins, Jace?' he growled.

Jace sucked at his cigar a few times to get it going. 'Nope,' he said at last. 'My money is all present and accounted for.'

Stonewall grunted & holstered his pistol. I noticed it was blue steel with a walnut grip.

A crowd of interested passers-by had stopped to gawp at us even though the wind was whipping up their coat-tails & skirts.

Jace took out his cigar & examined the glowing tip. 'Now that your pursuers have abandoned the chase,' he said, 'will you come inside and talk with me for a moment?'

I looked at his face, but I could not read it.

'Do I have a choice?' I said.

He tipped his head back & blew some smoke up in the air. 'No.'

'Then I will come with you.'

LEDGER SHEET 33

THE FASHION SALOON HAD SLATTED WOODEN HALF-doors that swung each way. Jace held open the right hand door & Stonewall the left. I took a deep breath & stepped inside. It was dim in there and it took my eyes a few moments to adjust after the brightness of the day outside. There was sawdust on the floor, but the strong wind had already blown it into a little drift against the end of a long bar along the right hand wall.

There were plain pinewood tables opposite the bar & also at the back of the room. Some of the tables were round & some were square. It smelled of stale beer & cigar smoke & sweat. A fat woman had a hurdy gurdy on her lap & she was cranking out a version of 'Camptown Races'. Three miners were dancing with some Hurdy Girls who had hardly any clothes on.

'Come on,' said Jace, who was halfway across the room. The sawdust was thicker here. It muffled the sound of my heavy shoes as I followed him.

Jace gestured towards a table near the back of the saloon, near a window with a 100-mile view. I could see the air outside was full of dust & a man's hat flew by.

Jace saw it, too. 'Danged Washoe Zephyr,' he said. He pulled out a chair for me.

I hesitated.

My Indian ma had taught me always to sit with my back against the wall so nobody could sneak up on me. But I did not think I had a choice this time, so I sat without protest. Jace sat opposite me. I observed that he had *his* back to the wall, and that he kept his hat on.

I heard a noise behind me and turned to see that the bar-keeper was closing a set of full-length inner doors. Once closed, those doors made the saloon quieter and calmer, but darker, too.

It made me feel trapped.

I reckoned Poker Face Jace had read the article in the newspaper & worked out who I was. Like everyone else, he wanted my *document of great value.*

'What'll you drink?' he said, taking the cigar from his mouth & tapping ash into a brass ashtray.

'Water,' I said.

Jace said, 'Nobody drinks the water here in Virginia. It is a mixture of arsenic, plumbago and copperas. It is only good for washing.'

'Coffee, then,' I said. 'Black coffee.'

'Stonewall?' said Jace. 'Bring us a pot of coffee and two cups and keep watch at the bar.'

'Yes, boss,' said the big man.

Jace looked at me & I looked back. Everything about him was straight. His nose was straight & his mouth was straight. Even his black eyebrows were straight.

I thought, 'What does he mean to do to me?'

He sucked his cigar & blew some smoke up towards the ceiling. 'You look familiar to me somehow. Have we met before?'

I did not know what to say, so I said nothing.

'You are inscrutable,' he said. 'I cannot tell what you are thinking.'

'That is my Thorn,' I said. My hands were cold & now that I was sitting down my knees were trembling.

'Beg pardon?'

'A Thorn in my side. I cannot understand what other people are feeling or thinking.'

Jace gave a small nod. 'I suppose that means you have trouble showing your own emotions.'

'Yes, sir. Also, sometimes I cannot recognize people I have met before. If they have grown a beard or their hair is different I get confused. Once, in Dayton, I walked right by my foster ma. She was wearing a brand new store-bought bonnet & I did not recognize her. Luckily she understood and was not too mad at me. It is a Thorn. A Thorn & a Curse.'

Jace tapped some more ash into the ash tray. 'What is your name?'

'P.K. Pinkerton,' I said. I figured he would find out anyway.

Jace's eyebrows went up. 'Related to Doc Pinkerton?'

'No. I am related to the famous Pinkerton Detectives of Chicago. Allan Pinkerton is my uncle. My pa was his brother Robert. I am going to Chicago to work for the Pinkerton National Detective Agency.'

'We never sleep,' said Jace.

It was my turn to say, 'Beg pardon?'

'That is their motto,' said Jace. 'On their signs and letterheads. The words "We Never Sleep" underneath an eye. They call themselves "Private Eyes".'

'I know they call themselves "Private Eyes",' I said. 'But I did not know about the motto.'

'Thank you, Stonewall,' said Jace, as the big man put a tin pot of coffee & two china mugs on the table. Stonewall filled both mugs, pushed one towards Jace, one towards me & then went to resume his position at the end of the bar.

My hands were still cold. I put them around the mug to warm them.

Jace rested his cigar in the ash tray & took a sip of coffee. 'P.K.,' he said. 'I believe what you call a Thorn & a Curse is really a Blessing. Furthermore, I think I can help you.'

'What do you mean: you can help me?' My hands around the coffee mug were a little warmer, but my knees were still trembling.

Jace picked up his cigar & took another suck. 'Have you ever heard of a card game called poker?'

'Yes, sir,' I said. 'I played it once or twice on the wagon train coming west.'

Jace nodded & exhaled smoke up into the air. 'How about faro and monte?'

'I have heard of them but I do not know the rules.'

'No matter. If you understand poker you can play those other games. Have you heard of a "poker face"?'

'Yes,' I said. 'It means not letting your face betray the cards in your hand.'

Jace sat forward & tapped the ash from his cigar into the ash tray. 'You are exactly right. A poker face means a face that expresses no emotion. No pleasure at getting a royal flush. Nor disappointment at getting a passel of small worthless cards. I have only once met a poker-player with a face as inscrutable as yours and he was an Indian.'

'I am half Sioux.'

'I suspected as much.' He sat back in his chair. 'You know, P.K., it has taken me years of training to achieve what you naturally have.'

I said, 'But a poker face is only useful if you can tell what other people are thinking. I know, because I played with those men once or twice and they always won.'

'Bravo,' said Jace. 'You are a very smart boy.'

'Yes, sir,' I said. 'I am smart. You show me something once I will never forget it. Also, I can do large sums in my head.'

Jace raised an eyebrow. 'What is 9 times 9?' he said.

I said, '81.'

'What is 30 times 22, with 10 subtracted & then divided by 5?'

I said, '130.'

'What is 138 times 3,567?'

I thought for a minute, seeing the numbers in my head. Then I said, 'Four hundred ninety two thousand two hundred forty six.'

He said, 'D-mn.' He glanced over at Stonewall and then looked at me for a moment. Then he reached into his breast pocket and pulled out a pack of playing cards. He shuffled them, dealt himself seven & fanned them out in his hand. He swiveled his wrist, showed me the hand for about the count of three & then put the cards face down on the table. 'What cards did I hold?' he said.

I said, 'Queen of Spades, 3 Hearts, 5 Diamonds, Queen of Diamonds, Jack of Clubs, 10 Spades & Ace of Spades.' As I named each card in order, he flipped it over to show I was right.

'D-mn,' said Jace again. 'You are an unmined vein, P.K. If I could train you to read what people are thinking, you would be the best card-sharp west of the Mississippi.'

I shook my head. 'I promised my dying ma that I would never kill a man or drink hard liquor or gamble.'

Jace stared at me for a while. I could not read his expression.

'And do you always keep your promises?' he said at last.

'I try.'

Jace looked over at Stonewall & shook his head. 'An honest genius, Stonewall. What a discouraging combination.' Stonewall grunted & took a sip of beer.

Jace put his cigar in his mouth & narrowed his eyes at me. 'Are you going to drink your coffee?' he said in his drawl. 'Or are you going to hug it all day?'

'I like it cold.'

Jace took the cigar out of his mouth. 'P.K.?' he said. 'What do you think is the most honest part of a man's body?'

'Beg pardon?'

'When you are trying to understand how a person is feeling, where do you look?'

'At their face.'

'A man's face is the most *dishonest* part of the body,' he said. 'Whereas the most honest part of a man's body is in fact the part furthest from his face.'

I said, 'His feet?'

Jace nodded. 'His feet.'

LEDGER SHEET 34

JACE GESTURED WITH HIS CIGAR. 'SEE THOSE MEN playing poker?'

I looked in the direction he had tipped his head. Four well-dressed men sat around a table. They might have been grocers, or clerks. One of them, a man with a pock-marked face, was dealing cards.

'Watch their feet,' said Jace.

I did. The men picked up their cards & examined them.

'See anything?'

I said, 'When they looked at their cards, they all moved their feet a little. Especially that bald man with the bushy mustache. His feet are kind of twitching.'

Jace nodded. 'His feet ain't just twitching; they're dancing. That man believes he has a winning hand.'

I said, 'You can tell that by his feet?'

'Of course,' said Jace. 'You only dance when you're happy.'

'Why is he letting his feet do that? Won't the other men see?'

'He is not aware that his feet are dancing. Nor are his friends. They are only concentrating on the parts above the table.'

I stared. It seemed hard to believe, but Jace was proved right a few minutes later when the bald man raked in the pile of coins. None of the men knew what their feet were getting up to under the table.

Jace put down his cigar & I felt the toe of one of his boots brush my shoes as he shifted in his chair & sat forward. He placed his cigar carefully in the shiny brass ashtray. 'Feet don't lie, P.K. When Stonewall brought you in here, I could tell you were afraid not by your face but by your feet. They were pointed away from me. When you sat down you hooked your ankles around the chair legs & sat on the edge of your seat. You warmed your hands on your coffee cup. When we are scared our hands get cold. But now your feet are pointing towards me, ain't they?'

I looked down at my feet. Sure enough, they were pointed towards Jace. How did he know that?

'How do you know that?' I said. 'You can't see my feet through the table.'

'A moment ago I very lightly touched the tips of your shoes with the toe of my boot. Did you feel it?'

I said, 'Yes. But I thought you were just shifting your

feet. What does it mean if my feet are pointed towards you?'

Jace almost smiled. 'It shows you are interested in what I am telling you.'

I stared down at my feet that were still pointing right towards him.

Jace was right. I was interested.

I was more than interested.

If he could help me understand people then maybe I could overcome my Thorn & become a good Detective & follow in my father's footsteps.

I looked back up at him.

Suddenly Jace leaned in close, so close that I could smell the coffee as well as the cigar smoke on his breath.

'The other sign you are giving now,' he said, 'is that the black part of your eyes just got a little bigger.' He sat back in his chair & looked at me from under the brim of his hat. 'That is something people cannot control. When a person gets excited or aroused then their pupils get a little bigger. When a person sees something they do not like, the pupils shrink. Most people do not notice such tiny clews. But I do.'

An idea struck me. 'Is that why you had me sit facing the window?' I said. 'So my face is lit up?'

He said, 'Bravo, P.K. With a little training, I can teach you to read other people as easy as I do.'

I said, 'But I promised my ma I would not gamble. It was her dying wish.'

Jace picked up his cigar & sucked. 'You told me that

before,' he said. 'And that suits me just fine. It means I won't have any competition.' He blew smoke up towards the ceiling. 'But what if you just helped me? Do you think your dead ma would object to that?'

I pondered this for a few moments. 'No,' I said at last, rubbing the back of my neck. 'I don't think she would mind.'

Jace smiled. 'When a person rubs the back of their neck like you just did,' he said. 'It often means they are not telling the whole truth.'

I stared at him. He was right. Ma Evangeline certainly *would* mind if I helped a person gamble. I had not even admitted that to myself and yet he had known it. I was struck with admiration.

Jace puffed his cigar. 'There might be such a thing as a "poker face",' he said, 'but there is no such thing as a "poker body". An example. See that lady over there? She is saying Yes but shaking her head No. Which do you think she really means?'

I said, 'No?'

He said, 'Correct. Her mouth is lying but her body is telling the truth.'

Jace put his feet right up on the table, ankles crossed & tipped his chair back so that the front legs were off the ground & his shoulders were leaning on the wall. He put his hands behind his head with the elbows out.

'This,' he said, 'is the posture of a confident boss. And this– ' here he tipped his hat down over his eyes, 'this is the posture of a relaxed person having a little nap. But really I am watching everything.'

I nodded. It did look like he was napping, but up close I could see his narrow black eyes scanning the room.

'Bring your chair round, P.K. Come sit by me,' he said. 'I am going to start our first lesson right here and right now.'

I looked at Poker Face Jace.

I needed to go to the Notary Public to get money for my Letter. But Jace had just offered to teach me how to understand people. I reckoned that was more important. I would give *anything* to learn what Jace knew. Even the Letter in my medicine bag.

LEDGER SHEET 35

I DRAGGED MY CHAIR NEXT TO **JACE'S &** SAT ON IT. Then I tipped it back & put my feet up on the table. I tried to shade my eyes like he was doing, but a plug hat does not have a wide enough brim.

'We'll start at the bottom and work our way up,' said Jace. 'I'll start your education with the most honest part of the body and end with the lyingest. And in return I want you to help me tonight. Is it a deal?' He reached his hand across his body to shake on it.

'It is a deal,' I said & shook his hand. His fingers were cool & firm & smooth.

'But first,' he said. 'I am going to show you something very simple that will open your eyes forever. See those men at the table? They are all smoking cigars. When a man blows the smoke up in the air, that shows he is feeling happy and confident. And if he blows his cigar smoke down, what do you think it means?'

'That he is not happy nor confident?'

'Correct. It means he is feeling insecure and unhappy. Also, the faster a man blows, the stronger his feelings are. If he blows smoke fast & down, he is probably angry. And if he blows smoke real slow down out of the corner of his mouth, well, that means he is very low.'

I stared at the men & saw immediately that he was right. I could not believe I had never observed something so simple & so true.

Over the next few hours, I did not think about my murdered pa & ma or my dead Indian ma or my dead Pinkerton pa. I did not think about Belle Donne or Isaiah Coffin or Dan De Quille or Titus Jepson. I did not wonder whether Walt & his boys were still staking out the Recorder's Office or whether the Notary Public was now closed for the day. I was too busy watching people.

I watched the men playing cards & blowing smoke up & sometimes down.

I watched the thirsty teamsters come to the bar & point their feet at the bartender as they ordered cool beer for their parched throats.

I watched the sweaty miners coming off their shift & I could tell who was friends with whom.

I watched more Hurdy Girls coming down from upstairs to relieve the miners of their hard-earned wages for just a dance or two. Jace showed me how to tell which ones really liked their partners & which ones were just bluffing. Some of them shook their heads No as they said Yes.

Afternoon became night & I did not notice.

The music was fine, but it did not entrance me.

I was entranced by Poker Face Jace, who was teaching me how to understand people.

He was opening a Door of Knowledge. It was like a Veil had been lifted from my eyes. The signs had been there all along, but I had never seen them. The trick, Jace said, was not to look at people's faces, but at their clothes & their props & their bodies & the way they stood. That afternoon we concentrated mostly on feet.

He taught me twelve things about how feet never lie. I did not write them down at that time, because I memorize things real fast, but I will write them down now for the benefit of whoever finds this record.

1. Feet are the most honest part of a person because we are not always aware of what our feet are doing.
2. If feet are set wide apart, the person is feeling strong & sometimes also angry.
3. If a person has the heel of one foot on the ground with the toes pointed up to the sky, he is happy.
4. If the feet get jiggly & do a little dance, the person is excited & happy.
5. If one foot starts twitching or kicking it shows the person is unhappy.
6. If a foot is tapping & there is no music that means the person is nervous or wants to go.
7. If someone's body is turned towards you but one or

both feet are not, they don't really want to be with you.

8. One or both feet sometimes point in the direction the person wants to go.
9. A person sitting with legs stretched out & ankles crossed is feeling relaxed & confident.
10. Ankles hooked around the chair leg show the person is nervous or trying to control himself.
11. People usually cross a leg towards a person they like.
12. Deliberately touching someone else's foot under the table is almost always a signal of some kind. Between a man & a woman it means desire.

When Jace told me this last rule I asked him what exactly he meant by 'desire'.

Jace asked Stonewall to bring him a whiskey & while he was at it to treat himself to one, too & he might as well get us a fresh pot of coffee & some cake.

Stonewall ordered the coffee, put a bottle of whiskey & three glasses on the table & then went off to find some cake. Jace filled one of the small glasses & offered it to me. When I shook my head he took a sip.

He said, 'P.K., do you know about men and women, and what they do together?'

I said, 'I have seen horses & dogs mating. And once a man and a woman behind the Dry Goods store in Temperance.'

'Well, sometimes it is about more than just mating.

There is desire.' He nodded towards a pretty Mexican woman who was coming downstairs. She was wearing a shimmery low-cut dress & a wave of men moved towards her like iron filings to a magnet.

'Oh,' I said. 'That kind of desire. Sparking.'

'Don't you ever feel desire?' said Jace.

'No,' I said. 'I think what men and women do together is stupid and strange.'

'How old are you?'

'Twelve.'

Jace sipped his whiskey. 'You'll feel different in a few years,' he said.

'No,' I said. 'I don't think so.'

Jace raised his eyebrows, then leaned forward & looked at me real hard.

'P.K., if you don't mind my asking: are you a boy or a girl?'

I stared at him.

Why was he asking me that question?

Nobody had ever asked me that before.

Was it because I had been dressed in pink gingham when he caught me and he had only just now recognized me?

Or was there another reason?

I glared at him.

Jace examined the tip of his cigar. 'The West can be a dangerous place for a girl. Here on the Comstock there are about a dozen men for every woman. Maybe more.' He gestured towards the woman in the sparkly dress.

'That's why girls like Mercedes over there get rich so quick. They can charge as much as they like for a dance. But a year from now she might be dead of too much dope or of despair or of having her throat cut, like poor Short Sally. They say one of her lovers cut her throat from jealousy,' he added, taking a pull from his cigar.

My mind was a jumble of things I could say to him, but I did not know which of them to speak out so I just fumed.

Jace blew the smoke down. 'A dozen men to one woman ain't natural. The papers claim we are all gentrified here in Virginia City, with our school and front gardens, our churches & charity balls, and our new piped water. But this is still a rough place for a woman. Or a girl.' Jace looked up at me. 'If I had a daughter I might consider dressing her up as a boy, just to keep her safe.'

At that moment, Stonewall came up with a fresh pot of coffee & refilled our mugs. A Chinese waiter appeared from behind him & put down three plates of vanilla layer cake. He gave us each a knife & fork & linen napkin.

Jace nodded his thanks to Stonewall, who had pulled up a chair.

I had finally decided what to say. 'There is a verse in Saint Paul's letter to the Galatians,' I began.

But Jace held up his hand to stop me. 'Don't you go quoting Scripture at me. Stonewall might tolerate it, but I won't.'

Stonewall kind of smiled & picked up his fork & dug into his piece of cake.

So did Jace.

He chewed thoughtfully for a few moments.

Then he winked at me. 'You may be a Freak of Nature, P.K. But you are a freak that is going to earn us both a lot of money.'

I thought, 'Money is good. But what you can teach me is worth all the gold & silver in the Comstock.'

LEDGER SHEET 36

LATER THAT NIGHT, POKER FACE JACE TOOK ME TO the New International Hotel, where he had a 'Sweet of Rooms'. We went towards the B Street entrance, and passed right by the Notary Public, which was shut up & dark.

The lobby of the International Hotel had Turkey carpets & potted plants & polished brass spittoons & frosted glass coal oil lamps on the wall. I was glad I was wearing my fancy 'tony bunch' get-up with my coat & plug hat.

At the desk, Jace asked the porter to have three meals sent to his Sweet. While he was ordering, I saw the big grandfather clock there & could not believe my eyes. It was nearly 11.00 oclock at night. The hours had whizzed by.

When we got to the room, all the lamps were lit. Jace took off his hat & jacket & hung them on pegs just inside the door. It was the first time I had seen him without his hat. His hair was gray at the sides & thinning on top. I realized he must be even older than Pa Emmet who had turned forty last year.

It was one of the nicest rooms I had ever seen. I took in the red velvet curtains & striped wallpaper & patterned carpets on the floor. There were polished wooden tables & velvet upholstered chairs & a marble fireplace & a brass spittoon. A balcony faced east over C Street. I went out there for a time, but the howling wind nearly tumbled me down into the canyon. If it had been light I knew a magnificent view of Virginia City & the surrounding country could be obtained. I reckoned that was why they called it a 'Sweet'. There were two bedrooms & I could see a mirrored wardrobe through the open door of one of them. The reflection showed a four-poster bed.

'Do you see what money can buy?' said Jace. He had poured some water from a jug into a washbasin & was splashing it on his face.

I said, 'I believe the iron work upon this house alone cost over $4,000.'

He patted his face dry with a linen towel & nodded. 'This is what they all aspire to.'

There was a soft knock on the door & Stonewall went to open it. A Chinaman in a spotless white apron brought our supper into the room on a narrow rolling table. He unfurled a white linen cloth & covered a square card table by the fire. Then he put out silver cutlery & last of all the plates of food. It was pork cutlets, mashed potatoes & greens with biscuits & butter. There were no hairs in the butter.

The three of us ate it sitting there by the warm fire. There was apple pie & cheese after, with black coffee. I was hungry & it was good. We ate in silence & that gave me a chance to look around the room & see all the nice things that money can buy. Jace's Sweet was bigger than our pine-log cabin in Temperance.

After we finished our pie, Jace sent Stonewall out with my key to Isaiah Coffin's studio.

As the door closed, Jace sat back in his chair & lit a cigar. 'What brings you to Virginia, P.K.?' he said.

I thought for a moment, wondering if I should tell him the Truth or not. But I wanted his knowledge more than I had ever wanted anything, so I said, 'My foster ma and pa were murdered yesterday and the killer is after me.'

His eyebrows went up. 'Who is the killer?'

'Whittlin Walt and two of his pards.'

'That is disturbing news.' Jace leaned over to one side so that he could tap ash into the fire. 'I have heard of Walt.' He sat back. 'Why Virginia City?'

'I was trying to get as far away from Walt as I could.'

'Did you succeed?'

'No. Walt and his pards are here in Virginia. They are still looking for me.'

'Why are they looking for you?'

I thought for a moment. Then I said, 'Because I know it was them that killed my foster ma & pa.'

He said, 'Now you are lying, P.K.'

I said, 'How could you tell?'

'The first time you paused, you were thinking whether you could trust me or not. Your eyes slid one way. The second time – just now – you were forming a lie and your eyes slid another way. Why is Walt after you?'

I wondered what he would do when he learned about my Letter. Then I decided it did not matter, as long as he kept teaching me what he knew.

'I have a Letter,' I said.

'Show me.'

I unbuttoned the top button of my starched shirt & pulled out my medicine bag. I noticed my hands were shaking a little as I opened it up. I handed my Letter to Poker Face Jace.

'Thank you, P.K.,' he said. He looked at me for a long moment & then unfolded the Letter. As he read it, I observed that his fingers were long & pale & tapered. The fingernails were real clean.

At last he folded the Letter & looked at me. 'I suppose they have told you that this could make you fabulously wealthy? That you will be a millionaire?'

'Yes,' I said. 'If it is not a forgery. I have to take it to the Notary Public on B Street to notarize it and then to the Recorder's Office to register it as mine. And then maybe to the judge.'

He said, 'I thought as much.'

Then he handed back the Letter. He did not seem interested in it. That surprised me.

He said, 'P.K.?'

'Yes, sir?'

'Don't fall in love with gold. Gold is a trap & a snare. Gold drives men mad and ruins families.'

'I thought they were mining silver here.'

'Silver. Gold. Same thing.'

'But *you* like silver & gold.'

'No. I like money. There is a difference.' He sucked on his cigar but it had gone out. He frowned at it. 'P.K., you just showed me that you are willing to trust me. As a reward, I am going to give you the best piece of advice you will ever get.'

'Yes?' I said. I realized I was sitting forward in my chair and I reckoned my pupils were big.

Poker Face Jace struck a match & held it up to the end of his cigar & sucked at it. He turned it until it was burning evenly.

'There are three types of people in this town,' he said. 'One: the big nabobs. They are the rich mine owners with responsibility for thousands of men. Two: the miners themselves. They risk their lives every day and their only hope of wealth is speculating. They are the stupidest. Three: the suppliers of goods and services. They are the smartest. They will prosper, but they will have to work hard.' Jace examined the end of his cigar. 'If you want to succeed in Virginia – or any other mining town – don't live off the mines, live off the people who live off the mines.'

I nodded. That made sense. Also, it fit with what Pa Emmet always said about Greed & Mammon.

Jace took a puff of his cigar & blew the smoke up. 'Then, of course, there's me,' he said. 'My job is to relieve all three types of their money.'

The door opened & Stonewall came in. He had retrieved my buckskins and moccasins from Isaiah Coffin's.

'Any problems?' asked Jace, going to the wardrobe and

pulling out a spare blanket. 'Any irate photographers or hurdy girls waiting in ambush?'

Stonewall shook his big head and handed me my own clothes. He also gave me back the key to the Photographic Studio. I put it in my medicine bag.

'I want you to put on your buckskins,' said Jace. 'And wear this blanket around your shoulders. Stonewall will take you to a nice two-bit saloon down on C Street.'

'What is a "Two-bit Saloon"?' I said.

'A two-bit saloon is where they make you pay 25 cents for a drink or a cigar, rather than half that, which is what you pay at a "bit house". Stonewall will show you where it is. Don't let on that you know him. Just follow him into the saloon and sit on the floor inside the door and keep your head down. You are going to pretend to be a Paiute beggar boy. But you will be looking at the feet of the men playing poker with me.'

Jace drained his coffee cup & examined it. It was a china teacup with pink & blue flowers on it.

'Stonewall,' said Jace, 'bring me the—'

But Stonewall was already there, holding out a tin cup.

Jace tipped his head towards me & Stonewall gave me the cup.

'Use that cup,' said Jace. 'If one of the men playing poker with me has dancing feet I want you to shake your cup so it jingles a little. Not a castanet, you understand. Just a little clink. Then put it back down on the ground with the handle pointing towards the man who holds the best cards. Like the needle of a compass. That will show me who has a good hand.'

'That is cheating,' I said.

'Not really,' said Jace, wiping his mouth & mustache with a napkin. 'If you were looking at his cards, that would be cheating.'

I thought about it. 'All right,' I said.

'If you see someone's foot kick out, or if he pulls his feet back beneath his chair, what will that mean?'

'That he has bad cards?'

'Most likely. In that case I want you to keep hold of the cup but make sure the handle points towards the man who is nervous. Got it?'

'Yes,' I said. 'Jingle for good hand, then cup on the floor. Keep it in my hand if someone is twitchy.'

'And remember to point the handle. But be discreet. Now, usually those two-bit saloons won't tolerate beggars but I gave one of the barmen a silver half-dollar and asked him to be nice to any Blanket Indians.'

I nodded to show I understood.

'If I think we are in danger of being discovered, I want you to vamoose. This will be my signal: I will untie this cravat from around my neck and tuck it in my front pocket. You can come back here, but don't let anybody see you. Stonewall will show you the tradesmen's entrance. Can you do that? Can you find your way back here if necessary?'

'Yes. I am real good at sneaking.'

'Good. Then go in the other room and put on those clothes.'

LEDGER SHEET 37

I WENT INTO JACE'S BEDROOM TO CHANGE.

It was real nice. It had a brass four-poster bed and a big wooden wardrobe and some striped wallpaper. I took off my high-tone trowsers and shirt and was glad to put on my own buckskins. The blanket was pale yellow & nicer than any blanket I had ever seen a begging Indian wear. But I dutifully wrapped it around my shoulders and went back out.

'Not bad,' said Jace, looking me up and down. 'But your face is too clean. Come here.'

I went over to him. He dipped the fingertips of his right hand into some cool ashes in front of the fire & then stroked them across my face. After a moment's consideration he added some ash smudges to the pale yellow blanket, too. 'That's better,' he said. 'But there's still something missing.'

He went to the hat stand & took down a black slouch hat with a hawk feather in the band.

'I won this off an Injun last week,' said Jace. 'Lucky I kept it.'

As I put on the hat, I caught a whiff of bear fat, which made me think of my Indian ma. The hat was slightly too big & came down over my eyes. So I took the folded WANTED poster from my medicine pouch & crumpled it up & stuck it up inside the crown of the hat & tried it on again. This time it did not impede my vision.

Jace nodded and blew smoke up. 'Go back in there and have a look at yourself in the mirror,' he said.

I went back into the bedroom and stood before a full-length mirror on the wall. I saw a grubby Blanket Indian with an expressionless face staring back at me. I noticed the eyes beneath the brim of the oversized hat were real dark, like Jace's, so you could not easily see the black part get bigger or smaller. What was the word Jace had used? Inscrutable.

I felt pleased at what I saw, but I noticed my expression did not change one whit.

'Stop admiring yourself,' said Jace from the doorway.

How could he tell? Then I noticed the toe of my right moccasin was pointing at the ceiling. I was not even aware of it. I dropped my foot and looked at Jace. He may have winked at me, but I could not be sure.

'Stonewall,' said Jace. 'Take P.K. down to Almack's. I will see you there in twenty minutes or so.'

Stonewall was sucking a lemon wedge. He tossed it into the fire & rose up out of his chair. Then he went to the coat rack & put on his coat & hat & gun belt.

I followed Stonewall out of the room. As we went along a plush corridor I said, 'Would you really have blown my brains out today?'

He stared at me with his left eye. His right eye was looking somewhere else.

He said, 'Course not. I was just trying to scare you into giving me any gold pieces you might of stole off Jace.'

I nodded. That made me feel a little better.

'Why are you called "Stonewall"?' I said.

'Do you know who Stonewall Jackson is?' he said in his growly voice.

'Yes,' I said. 'He is a famous general in the Reb army.'

Stonewall said, 'He is a military genius. I call myself after him because I do not like my real name.'

'I don't like my real name neither,' I said.

Stonewall grunted & opened an unmarked white door. Narrow stairs led down & we emerged right onto the boardwalk of C Street.

It was after midnight now but it seemed even busier than during the hours of daylight. I saw lots of bearded miners and I judged they had just got off their shift.

The wind was still blowing and it was cold now. I was glad of the yellow blanket and the oversized hat. I tied the two corners of the blanket around my neck and then threw one of the free corners over my shoulder so I was well-wrapped. Then I hurried after Stonewall.

The crowds parted before him & I found that if I followed in his wake I did not get jostled or stepped on once. Everywhere people were shouting & laughing.

Once I thought I heard gunshots followed by screams and then laughter. Through the thin soles of my moccasins I could feel the boardwalk throbbing. Even in the middle of the night the stamps pounded the quartz.

We stopped on the northwest corner of C Street & Taylor, near the hardware store with the coffee-pots & stove on top. Catty corner across the intersection was a fine looking stone building. Torches on either side of the door lit up a big sign that read: Almack's Oyster & Liquor Saloon. We crossed Taylor & then Stonewall turned his ugly head. I wasn't sure whether he was looking at me or not because his eyes pointed in two different directions. He said in a low voice, 'When I go into the saloon you follow me in, but sit by the door like Jace told you.'

I nodded & watched Stonewall cross the street & go in.

Almack's Oyster & Liquor Saloon did not have swinging wooden doors like the saloon where I had sat with Jace all afternoon. This one had proper double doors with brass handles & frosted glass panels above, each engraved with the word ALMACK'S. Stonewall did not close the door all the way, so I was able to slip in silently.

It was dim & smoky in there, just like the Fashion Saloon. But one glance showed me the difference between a bit house and a two-bit saloon like this. There was striped wallpaper on the walls & colored shades on the lamps & two chandeliers hanging from the ceiling. The floor-boards were polished & waxed so that the scent of honey was mixed in with the smell of beer, lamp-oil

& cigars. I sat cross-legged near a potted fern, with my back against the wall & my tin cup in front of me.

In the far corner to my left was a low stage with a bearded bald man playing a banjo. He was playing a popular song about a girl called 'Lorena'. He made it sound sad & hopeful at the same time. I had to pinch myself not to be entranced.

To my right was the bar. Stonewall was standing there with one boot up on the brass foot rail. When he saw me come in, he turned to the barman and said something to him. The barman glanced at me and then nodded.

There was a big mirror behind the bar & either side of it hung a blackboard. The blackboards looked like the ones in my Dayton schoolhouse, with letters & marks on them. I can read but I could not decipher the code on those blackboards.

It was pretty crowded. I noticed the men at the bar were mainly drinking & those at the tables were mainly playing cards. An inner door showed a glimpse of the Restaurant where oysters were served. There was a sound of laughter & talking and every so often someone would spit into a brass spittoon. There were some women in there, too. They wore bright-colored dresses with lace & ribbons and low cut necks.

My foster pa would be Turning in his Grave, if they had buried him yet.

LEDGER SHEET 38

WHILE I WAITED FOR JACE TO COME IN I WATCHED some men playing poker at a square table. It was like a Veil had been lifted from my eyes. I could see who was nervous & who was happy & who was bluffing. Above the table they revealed almost nothing. But their legs & feet betrayed them every time they shifted in their seats.

It was hard to believe they were not aware of it. But then I remembered I had not been aware of my feet till Jace told me.

The doors on my right swung open & my nose detected a familiar stench as two men came in. Even above the smell of lamp oil, floor wax & expensive cigars I recognized that dead-critter pipe tobacco. It was Sam Clemens from the Territorial Enterprise & a high-tone man with a plug hat & walking stick. Sam scanned the room & although he saw me, he did not give me a second look. That told me my disguise was a good one.

The two of them went over to the bar.

'Good evening, Mr. Goodman,' said the bar-keeper.

'Good evening, Lorry,' said Goodman. He was young & tall, with a round face & dark mustache. 'This here's our new Local, Sam Clemens.'

'Pleased to meet you,' said the bar-keeper. 'What'll you have?'

'Two beers,' said Mr. Goodman. 'Mark twain.'

The bar-keeper nodded & chalked up two lines on a blackboard under the initials JG.

'What's that about, Joe?' said Sam Clemens. He was looking at the blackboard.

Joe Goodman said, 'If you can talk the bartender into letting you take drinks on tick, then you can settle your account weekly. That means when you come in you just tell him to mark one or mark twain or however many you are ordering.'

'They say that on riverboats, too,' said Sam Clemens.

'Beg pardon?'

'I used to be a Riverboat Pilot on the Mississippi. "Mark twain" meant the water was two fathoms deep.'

'Is that a fact?' said Joe Goodman.

'It is indeed,' said Sam Clemens. 'I never thought I would be saying those words on a mile-high mountainside with a landscape like a singed cat.'

Joe Goodman chuckled & lifted his beer. 'I hope you will say those words on many occasions, especially when I am with you.' They clinked glasses & they both drank deeply.

The banjo player was playing one of those fancy pieces that races along faster than a driverless stage. When he finished, everyone clapped.

I heard Sam Clemens say, 'A fellow who can play like that can surely be depended upon in any kind of a musical emergency.'

Joe Goodman chuckled again & then stopped. I saw him look towards the door. Everyone else looked, too, including the banjo player, who had not yet started his next song.

I kept my head down, but I saw Poker Face Jace's polished black leather boots come into view.

As Jace went over to the bar I looked up from under the brim of my hat. I saw him order a glass of brandy & everybody started talking again. The two reporters were staring at him & Joe Goodman leaned in & whispered something in Sam Clemens's ear. He was speaking too soft for me to hear.

One of the Hurdy Girls went up to Jace. She wrapped her bare arms around his neck & tried to kiss him full on the lips. He smiled & turned his head so that she gave him a kiss on the cheek instead. Then he unwrapped her arms from his neck & patted her rump & took his glass & went over to one of the tables.

Jace said something to the men sitting there. He was still smiling. One of the seated men smiled back & nodded & scooped up his winnings & left. He went to the bar to buy a drink & his upward pointed toe showed that he was pleased Jace had taken his seat.

It was a good seat: the kind I knew Jace liked. Now he was sitting with his back against the wall, facing me. He was under an oil lamp & the brim of his flat black hat threw his face into shadow.

I thought that was clever. The men he was playing with couldn't see his eyes, but he could see theirs.

My heart was beating fast. Would our plan work?

I watched while one of the men dealt out the cards. The critical moment would be when they first saw their cards. I watched the men's feet intently, but with my head still down. As soon as they fanned out their cards, their feet shifted. The man with his back to me planted his feet firmly on the floor. The one to my left pointed his towards the door. The one to my right tapped his heels & the toe of one boot pointed briefly up.

I rattled my cup, just a little, then put it down with the handle pointing to the man on my right, with his back to the bar. He had droopy eyes & sagging skin. He reminded me of a bloodhound.

Sure enough, Bloodhound had a good hand & he won the pot. Jace was gracious & complimented him. As they played, Jace told stories in his pleasant Southern drawl. His face remained expressionless, but his eyes had a kind of smile about them, even when he was losing. Over the next hour or two I saw that although he seemed to be losing as often as the others, his pile of coins was growing steadily. I noticed some of the men pointed their feet towards him. They did not seem to mind him relieving them of their money. Once he called Stonewall over and had him bring the whole table a bottle of whiskey. But I noticed that he barely touched his own drink.

As the night progressed, I jingled my cup and pointed the handle & I saw the pile of coins growing before Jace. He was doing well. Men came & went & after about four hours there were three different men at the table with Jace.

It must have been real late, for I was stifling yawns. A shift of miners had just come off duty and it was as crowded in there as when we had arrived. There were two different bar-keepers on duty now & an accordion player had replaced the banjo. I guessed most saloons in Virginia stayed open 24 hours.

Jace had not moved from his seat against the wall all night. To his left & my right was a man with a sage-brush sized beard who called himself a 'speculator'; he had his back to the bar. Next – with his back to me – was a man with a gold pocket watch who worked for Wells Fargo. On Jace's right sat a Mine Supervisor with a tobacco-stained mustache.

As the game progressed, I realized the Wells Fargo man took out his watch every time he had a bad hand. The mine supervisor whistled under his breath when he had a good hand. The Speculator spat whenever he was disgusted with a hand or with anything else. You might think such 'tells' would be obvious but none of the others seemed to notice.

I think Jace & I would not have realized these things so clearly without the men's feet betraying their true feelings.

I noticed that sometimes Jace ignored my signals &

as a result he lost the hand. It made me think of Pa Emmet when he was first teaching me chess. He would purposely make a bad move & lose & when I asked him why, he said it was so I would not get discouraged. I reckoned Jace was doing the same thing.

People gave me peanuts, wooden matches or even coins as they exited the saloon. I ate the peanuts & put the matches in my pocket but left the coins to keep the cup jingly. One or two people spat on me as they left. But mostly the people ignored me & I ignored them.

But it was hard to ignore Whittlin Walt when he strode into Almack's Oyster & Liquor Saloon. His two men were with him: Extra Dub with the big Adam's Apple & Whiny Boz with the squinty eye and nose broken by me. The accordion player stopped wheezing away at his instrument and for the second time that night the whole place went quiet. I saw Stonewall appear out of the shadows near the bar. He was watching them along with everyone else.

Walt & his pards ordered a bottle of whiskey & then turned to survey the crowd.

I froze.

Walt was looking for a 12-year-old dressed as an Indian. I had eluded him by dressing as a little girl, a Celestial & a member of the tony bunch. But now I was dressed like an Indian again. He had seen through my disguise once. Would he see through it again?

Apparently not. He downed his whiskey and turned back to pour another.

Extra Dub and Boz did not recognize me either,

thanks to my grubby blanket and big slouch hat.

Walt knocked back his second glass of whiskey & said, 'Order yourselves another, boys. On me.' Then he grasped the whiskey bottle by the neck & he went over to Jace's table.

'Move,' he said to the Mine Supervisor, and he spat some tobacco juice near the man's feet.

The Mine Supervisor looked up at Walt. He opened his mouth & then closed it again. In silence he collected his winnings & went to the bar.

The downward direction of his cigar smoke told me he was not happy.

Walt took his place. Now he was sitting facing the bar, side on to me. I could see his whole body from his ugly face to his big, spurred boots under the table. His jaw was working on a chaw of tobacco & as I watched he turned towards me & spat. But he still did not notice me.

Everybody in the room was armed with a Colt's Navy Revolver at the very least. Walt had the larger caliber Army Revolver & that Bowie Knife stained with the blood of a dozen men & women.

'What are we playing?' said Walt. The man with the accordion had paused and though people had started talking again, it was still quiet enough that I could hear Walt chewing.

'Poker. Five card draw,' said Jace, who was shuffling the cards. He was fast & thorough & he did not show off, like some dealers.

Walt spat into the spittoon, poured himself a glass of whiskey & tossed it down in one.

Jace was still shuffling. 'You're Whittlin Walt, ain't you?' he said. 'I have heard of you.' I couldn't see his eyes clearly but I thought he might be looking over at me.

'I have heard of you, too,' said Walt. 'Jason Francis Montgomery, sometimes known as Poker Face Jace.' Walt took out his fearsome Bowie Knife & cut a fresh plug. 'If you cheat, I will whittle you to the size of a toothpick.'

'I never cheat,' said Jace in a pleasant tone of voice. 'I have been known to bluff on occasion, but I never cheat.'

Walt snorted and sheathed his big knife.

The Wells Fargo bank man chuckled. I was surprised he did not make a citizen's arrest as there was a WANTED poster behind the bar beside one of the blackboards. I glanced over at Sam Clemens & Joe Goodman. But the space they had been occupying all night was now empty.

Jace dealt a few hands & I watched Walt carefully. The first thing I noticed about him was that he was left-handed. The second thing I noted was that his feet were as revealing as anyone else's. The third thing I noticed was that whenever he was bluffing or nervous, he would sit real still & stop chewing his tobacco. Once I was pretty sure he swallowed when he meant to spit.

They had played a few hands & Jace was dealing, when it happened.

Jace said, 'What brings you to Virginia, Walt?'

Over in the corner the accordion was playing 'Alice Where Art Thou?' but not too loud. I could hear what they were saying all right.

Walt turned his head & spurted some tobacco juice

into the spittoon & said, 'I am searching for a kid name of Pinkerton. Any of you seen him?'

I thought my heart had stopped.

Jace put in a silver dollar. 'Ante up,' he said as he shuffled one last time. Everybody put in a coin.

'Allan Pinkerton,' said the sage-bearded Speculator as he watched the cards fall. 'I hate that son of a blank.'

'Why's that?' said Jace.

'He sells himself to the Union generals faster than one of Hooker's Hurdy Girls.'

'Well I for one am glad of the Pinkertons,' said the Wells Fargo man as he examined his cards. 'Their Stagecoach Detectives have cut our thefts by half.'

'I hear he had a brother,' said Jace, putting down the pack to examine his own cards. 'Name of Robert.'

'Yeah,' said the Speculator. 'That Robert Pinkerton is an ongoing pain in my butt.'

'You knew him?' said Jace.

'You talk like Robert Pinkerton's dead,' said the Speculator, re-arranging his cards.

'Ain't he?' said Jace.

'Not unless he went and got himself kilt in the last two months,' said the Speculator.

I was so startled by this statement that I jumped to my feet. Could it be that my original pa was alive?

LEDGER SHEET 39

I COULD NOT BELIEVE WHAT I HAD JUST HEARD IN Almack's Oyster & Liquor Saloon.

The sage-brush bearded Speculator claimed to have seen my father only two months ago. Luckily only Jace took any notice of my reaction. He made a small patting gesture, and I knew he meant 'sit down'.

I sat down.

The sage-brush bearded Speculator tossed two gold $20 pieces into the center of the table & everybody stared for a moment.

The Wells Fargo man whistled. 'That's rich,' he said.

'My last hand,' said the Speculator.

The other three each put in two gold coins.

The Speculator put a pair of cards face down on the green table & slid them across. 'Two cards,' he said.

Jace gave him two.

The Wells Fargo man put down three cards. 'Three,' he said.

Jace gave him three.

Walt threw down two cards.

Jace gave him two.

Walt leaned forward & said, 'I know for a fact that Robert Pinkerton is alive and well and living in Chicago. But it ain't him I'm interested in. It's that kid. Got something belongs to me.'

Jace put down a card & dealt himself a fresh one.

'Was that the kid who robbed & kilt his foster parents?' said the Speculator, putting down 3 gold coins.

My hands were trembling, making my cup rattle, so I gripped it tight to make it stop.

'I fold,' said Wells Fargo, & added, 'I read about that kid in the paper. They say he's half Injun.'

'You can't trust Injuns of any description,' snorted Walt as he saw the bet of $60. 'I keep telling people that, but they don't listen.'

Jace added his 3 gold pieces to the others. 'I hear it was a set-up job. I hear the kid was innocent.'

Walt spat tobacco juice onto the floor. He did not even aim for the spittoon. 'What do you have?' he asked the Speculator.

'Full house, sevens high,' said the bushy bearded man, laying out his cards on the table.

'Full house, Kings high,' said Jace. He prepared to scoop up his winnings but Walt put his own cards down.

'Four ladies,' said Walt, by which I believe he meant four

Queens. He pulled a lot of coins over to his part of the table.

Now until this hand, Jace had been $720 up on the evening. More than half a year's pay for a newspaperman. I looked down at my tin cup. The handle was pointing towards Walt. My fearful heart had caused Jace to lose over $100 in one hand.

That was my fault. I had not been paying attention to their feet. I had been too caught up in their talk of my dead pa who was apparently alive & well & living in Chicago.

And now Jace had lost badly.

I saw Jace looking at me. I could not read his expression.

'What are you looking at?' said Walt. He turned his head & his gaze swept over me. I quickly lowered my head, but for a second our eyes had locked.

'Hey, Dub,' said Walt. 'Look at that filthy Blanket Injun kid begging over there. Since when does Almack's Oyster & Liquor Saloon allow beggars?'

'Since never,' said Extra Dub in his raspy voice. He took his foot off the bar rail. 'I think that's the kid we're looking for.'

'I think so, too,' said Boz. 'Got those cold eyes.'

I kept my head down & pretended not to understand.

But the accordion player had stopped playing & the whole saloon had gone quiet. I could feel them all staring at me.

'Hey you!' said Walt. 'Hey, Digger Injun! Is your name Pinky?'

I kept my head down & my eyes fixed on his feet. I heard Walt's chair scrape against the polished floor & as he stood up I could see that his spurred boots were pointing towards me.

Then I heard Jace's drawl, 'Stop right there or I'll fill you with balls,' he said.

I looked up to see that Jace was on his feet & was aiming a Colt's Pocket Pistol right at Walt's heart. It was a .32 caliber, bigger than mine but not as big as Walt's. 'Stop right there,' Jace repeated. He had stretched out his right arm to take careful aim. He had his side on to Walt but he was now facing the bar.

Walt froze for a moment & then gave a kind of smile. He knew his back was covered. Extra Dub & Boz Burton were both pointing their pieces at Jace.

'Watch out, Jace!' I cried, but it was too late. Dub's gun went off at the same time as someone else's. I saw Jace go down, hit in the chest. Then everything was confused & seemed to happen at once. I heard the deafening report of Stonewall's Le Mat and guessed he was firing at Extra Dub because the bar-keep had grasped Boz's arm so that his revolver was now firing into the ceiling. Plaster dust was raining down & a woman was screaming & chairs scraped as men got up to flee.

But I was not really paying attention to any of those things.

Whittlin Walt was coming towards me with purpose & intent, his Bowie Knife in his left hand.

I am ashamed to say I forgot all about the Smith & Wesson's seven-shooter in my pocket. I turned tail and ran like a yellow dog.

LEDGER SHEET 40

MY EARS WERE RINGING WITH THE SOUND OF gunshots as I ran outside. I saw that it was dawn & that the boardwalk was jammed with people watching a procession. The wind was flapping their garments & now that I was outside I could hear a brass band above the Zephyr's howling. I pushed through people and as I jumped down off the boardwalk I nearly got shmooshed by a horse-drawn fire engine draped in black cloth. Firemen in their fire helmets & red flannel shirts & shiny black belts were walking down the middle of the street. Why were they congregating here so early? Had they come to taunt me? They were blocking my escape.

The wind was buffeting me and making my blanket flap behind me like a cape. It threw dirt in my eyes & filled my mouth with dust. The brass band was getting closer & louder.

I darted between another black-draped fire engine &

some firemen. The boardwalk opposite was a solid wall of miners so I could not jump up. I had to run along the street, against the stream of traffic. Firemen cursed me as I jostled them but I could barely hear above the sound of the brass band & the still-howling wind. As soon as I reached a side street I turned up it. It was crowded with miners, too, but I managed to shove through the press of bodies.

I encountered the brass band up on B Street, also a shiny black funeral coach pulled by coal-black horses with black plumes nodding from their foreheads. Only then did I remember that today was the day of Short Sally's funeral. That must be why all those miners were filling the boardwalks: to watch the procession. I shoved through more miners up another street & I finally found myself up on A Street which was mercifully deserted.

I felt sick & had to stop then & rest my hands on my knees. My foster ma & pa were dead, just like Short Sally. Jace was probably dead, too: shot in the heart because of me. So many dead people. And yet the pa I always believed dead was really alive. He had just never bothered to track me down.

I was still gasping for breath when something like a Wasp whined past my ear. But it was not a Wasp.

It was a Bullet fired by Walt.

He had emerged from the crowds a half block below me & he was shooting at me with his big Colt's Army Revolver. The sun had still not risen but it was light enough for him to get off a shot that had almost killed me.

I ran up between two buildings & at the same time I pulled my seven-shooter out of my pocket.

I stopped & peered out from behind a shed & saw Walt emerging from the alley. I got off a shot. You could hardly hear my piece above the moaning of the wind. I don't think he even noticed.

A startled pair of quail went flapping up out of a clump of sage as I backed into it. My stomach sank as I realized I was nearing the outskirts of the town. The sun was just rising from behind the far eastern mountains. If I went any higher I would be exposed on the mountainside by its bright rays.

Then I saw the big white building of the Mexican Mine further up the sage-dotted slope. Its stamps were silent & no smoke came from its tall chimney.

I ran towards it.

I thought, 'There will be plenty of nooks & crannies to hide in there.'

But when I got there, panting & nearly sick from running in thin air, I found it was locked as tight as a Wells Fargo safe.

The sun was up now and it glinted off narrow metal tracks leading up the side of the mountain to a dark square in the mountainside. The tracks were for a mine car and the dark square was the entrance of the Mexican Mine itself.

The wind was howling at me & the sun was pointing me out with bright rays.

I thought, 'If I can just get somewhere dark & quiet, I can think what to do.'

219

I ran up towards the mine entrance, chasing my own long shadow with its flapping cape of a blanket and feathered hat.

The entrance of the Mexican Mine was open but deserted. I reckoned the miners had all been given the morning off for Short Sally's funeral. There were half a dozen candles lying on a raw wood table at the entrance. I shoved all six of them into my right-hand pocket so Walt wouldn't have any light to chase me. I put down my seven-shooter for just a moment, in order to light one of the candles on the oil-lamp hanging in the entrance. In my haste, it did not even occur to me to take the oil-lamp along with those candles.

I made another bad mistake at that moment but did not realize it until later.

Holding up the candle, I hurried between the tracks & down the empty tunnel as it went deeper & deeper into the mountain. My single flickering candle lit the way.

It was getting darker & darker.

I turned & looked back & I could no longer see daylight.

I slowed down & tried to listen for signs of pursuit. The terrible howling Zephyr was silenced in here, but the blood swooshing in my ears was almost as loud.

For a while there were coal oil lamps in wall niches along the way, then there was nothing. And still I was going into the side of the mountain.

I must have gone 200 feet, maybe more, when I saw a dark shape looming up ahead just outside the dim & flickering light of my candle.

Then I heard something snorting. Something big.

With a trembling hand, I held up my candle.

I could see the gleaming milky eyes of some demonic creature.

I nearly died of fright right then & there. I almost dropped my candle but then I heard a horse's snort.

It was a black pony.

She was harnessed to a whim & I suppose on a working day she went round & round hoisting ore from the infernal regions below. But today she was just standing there.

'Hey, girl,' I said. 'Don't be afraid.'

My voice sounded small as it echoed in the tunnel.

The pony rolled her eyes. She was not comforted by my fearful reassurance.

I went forward & stroked her flank. Her coat was coarse & dusty, her eyes milky in the light of my candle.

I think she had been down in the dark for so long that she was almost blind.

I gave her a final pat & I moved cautiously forward. My feeble light showed a continuation of the tunnel behind her and also several massive caverns. There were three of them, their walls glittering with quartz. But none of them went more than 20 or 30 feet in. I could see where they ended.

It was warm in there. But it was not a cozy warmth. It was a smothering warmth, like a stifling blanket over your face & nose. Also the air was clammy. It made my skin prickle all over.

Then I felt more prickling as the echo of voices further back along the tunnel raised all the little hairs on the back of my neck.

Someone had followed me into the Mexican Mine.

I needed to go further in.

I held up my flickering candle.

Then I saw it. A ladder sticking up from a hole in the ground.

I went cautiously towards it.

It was a black pit in the middle of black earth.

In the feeble light of my candle, I could not even see the bottom.

Just the rungs going down into blackness.

I looked back towards the entrance & the poor horse standing & waiting to go round & round. I ran back to her & put my candle on a ledge of quartz. Then I undid her shackles with fumbling fingers & pointed her back the way I had come & slapped her rump.

'Go on, girl.' I hissed. 'Go give Walt a fright. Git.'

The pony obediently trotted off towards the exit. I knew a black horse emerging from the tunnel wouldn't kill Walt, but it might scare the bejeezus out of him & maybe send him back out into the light of day.

That is where I wished I was: in the light of day.

But I knew I had to keep going until the miners came back & it was safe.

I clamped the candle between my teeth & flung my blanket cape back to free my arms & started down the ladder as fast as my flickering flame would allow me. I had to cock my head at an angle so I wouldn't singe the brim of my hat. That threw me off balance a little & made the going tricky.

You would have thought it would get cool & clammy deep down in the earth. But as I descended it got hotter & hotter. I had to stop & take the candle out of my mouth & wipe away drool & breathe properly for a while. Then I sent up a prayer & replaced the candle in my mouth & carried on down.

When at last I reached the bottom of the ladder, I was so relieved that my knees could not hold me & I had to sit for a spell.

Then I looked around & for a moment astonishment replaced terror.

If you have ever seen the timber frame of a house before the walls are on, imagine that as far as the eye could see. A hundred big cubes, made of square planks almost as big as me & twice as tall, all stretched away into the darkness before & behind & above & below. I must have been a hundred feet deep & yet somehow they had brought a whole forest of timbers down here.

As I held my candle up & looked around, the little yellow flame showed me I could go deeper still. There was a narrow staircase like a corkscrew, spiraling down into the hot, clammy darkness.

It was the last place on earth I wanted to go.

It was like going down into the Fiery Pit of Hell itself.

But only a stretch of tunnel & that ladder separated me from Walt & I knew I had to go down.

At least I did not have to clamp the candle between my teeth, but as I went down & down, I felt as if I was in one of those nightmares where you fall real slow. All around me was a framework of wood and though I knew the timbers were thick it seemed they were only toothpicks holding up a whole mountain. After maybe 15 minutes of dizzy descent, I finally reached solid ground.

I was amazed to see a whole city down here. There were picks & axes & a small saw-mill & lanterns. I also saw wheelbarrows half full of ore, ready to take their loads to buckets attached to windlasses & ropes & pulleys. I realized on any other day this place would be swarming with miners.

As it was, it was swarming with rats.

Rats make good eating if you are desperate. But there were too many of them down here for my liking.

When they saw my light they melted into the shadows. But I knew they were there. I could see their beady red eyes glinting at me.

As I went closer to the rock wall, I saw what must be the Mother Lode.

The Comstock Ledge.

The Vanilla Frosting in the Cake of Mount Davidson. In the light of my candle it was sparkling quartz all veined with blue, like the marble pillars at the International Hotel. I knew those blue veins were silver & that they would have to be pounded & sieved & amalgamated & refined. But it was silver & it was thick. It was what drove men & women mad.

224

Suddenly I was dizzy and panting for breath; the blanket tied round my neck was choking me. I untied it & re-tied it more loosely & soon felt a little better. I wondered if anybody ever smothered down here.

Then I held up my candle with my right & went all round the wall-rock. I heard the rats scuttling & squeaking but they kept out of sight. I had been looking for a good place to hide for maybe ten minutes when I felt a hot damp draft on my face.

I was about to offer up a silent prayer of thanks for a breeze, even a hot one, when without warning the candle in my hand was snuffed out & I was plunged into darkness darker than the inside of a black steer on a moonless night.

I WAS 200 FEET BELOW GROUND IN A RAT-INFESTED mine & it was darker than a tar pit at midnight.

Then I remembered that at Almack's Oyster & Liquor Saloon some people had tossed matches in my begging cup as a cruel joke.

I started fishing around in my pocket.

That was when I realized I did not have my seven-shooter.

I went cold all over. I remembered I had put it down at the mouth of the mine tunnel so I could light a candle. A candle that had just been extinguished.

I could picture my seven-shooter lying there, right where I left it.

I was without light & without the protection of a firearm.

If there was ever a time to pray, it was then. I said, 'Oh Lord, please help me.'

I took a breath & dug my fingers deep into my right hand pocket where I had put the matches. I felt a small hole & I realized most of the matches must have fallen out.

'Please Lord,' I prayed.

At last my fingers encountered half a match down one corner of my pocket.

I felt it all over & my heart sank.

It was the wrong half.

I could hear the rats scuttling closer to me in the darkness as I dug deeper in my pocket.

Finally, right down in the bottom of my pocket, stuck between two stitches, was the sparkable half of the match.

That half-match was the only chance I had of illuminating the darkness. I carefully pulled it out of my pocket. Then, holding the candle in my left hand & the match in my right, I tried to strike it against the damp rock face.

The first time I tried, nothing happened.

I could hear the rats coming closer.

The second time I tried to strike it, nothing happened.

I felt a rat run over my moccasin.

Finally on the third try the half-match flamed up.

I brought the flame to the candle's wick, but my hands were shaking so bad I feared I would not get them to meet. Just as the match-flame was beginning to burn my fingers, the wick of the candle caught, flickered, steadied & burned bright.

The rats scuttled away & I breathed a sigh of relief so great that it almost blew out the candle again. I carefully cupped my hand around the flame to protect it.

Then I moved forward.

I felt the hot, damp draft again: the one that had blown out my candle. It was coming up from a tunnel in one of the bluest parts of the rock face. Cherishing my flame, I carefully started down this dark passageway. There were some picks & hammers beside the walls of the tunnel, which was shored up with timbers like a row of sash window frames stretching away into the earth.

The tunnel went down a gentle grade for maybe a quarter mile. Every so often I caught the faint scent of alkali water. Ma Evangeline once told me there were 2000-foot shafts in some of the mines of the Comstock.

The damp got damper & the heat got hotter & at last I came into a clammy chamber about twelve foot by twelve. Here the tunnel ended. And here the scent of alkali was strongest.

I wondered where the smell was coming from so I held up my candle, being careful to protect it with my hand. Its yellow light showed several objects in the cave.

A wooden crate.

Four wooden buckets, three of them upturned.

A coffee-pot.

Empty tin cans. (Small ones; not the big oyster cans.)

A shovel, pickaxe & hammer leaning up against one wall.

An empty bottle of whiskey.

I took a cautious step forward & almost tripped over a little wooden sign stuck in the ground.

It read DANGUR.

I felt sick & dizzy when I saw what lay beyond it. A gaping black hole about six feet wide that seemed to me the very mouth of Satan.

I WENT CAUTIOUSLY TO THE LIP OF THE PIT & looked down. It was so deep that I could not see the bottom. I caught a whiff of alkali & remembered that Ma Evangeline had also told me that some shafts dropped down to rivers of boiling water running through the mountain. That is why it is so hot down here. There is a river of boiling water running beneath Virginia City.

A sudden moist gust from the shaft almost blew out my candle again, so I lit a second one from the first & I held them both close to my body, sheltering them from any disaster. Then, carefully avoiding the bottomless pit, I went to investigate the crate in the corner.

It had words stamped on the side: N.B. JACOBS FINE OLD CORN WHISKEY, SAN FRANCISCO, CAL.

Bringing my candles closer, I could see the crate was half-full of unopened whiskey bottles. On top of the crate lay three half burnt candles, a pack of cards, a piece of moldy cheese & some blank pages of a ledger book, all swollen with steam from the pit. There were also some matches.

Matches! Hallelujah! I put some in my medicine bag so I would not be plunged into darkness again.

Beside the crate were the three upturned buckets, one of which I am using to sit on as I write. I figured some of the miners came in here to have whiskey & a snack & play poker for matches. It was their own miniature subterranean saloon. I could not explain the pages from the ledger book. Maybe they used them to keep a tally while they were playing cards.

It is not drafty here in the corner, only at the mouth of the cave, so I dripped a bit of wax on the wooden lid of the crate & stuck one of my burning candles there. Then I took the other candle & continued investigating this cave. There was a fourth bucket over by the pit. My nose told me it had been used as a latrine bucket. Presumably the men who came here used it & then emptied it out into the Pit.

One good thing about this dank, hot cave is that the rats do not seem to like it. I put the coffee-pot under a drip from the stony ceiling. I get about an inch of water an hour. It is that poisonous mixture of arsenic, plumbago & copperas Belle warned me about. But I am going to be dead soon so I reckon it don't matter.

I got hungry a while ago so I took out my medicine bag to get my Indian ma's flint knife. I cut the mold off the cheese & ate it.

I soon got hungry again & ate the moldy bit. I could now eat whang leather with gusto.

Short Sally's funeral must be long over because I have felt the throbbing of the Quartz Stamp Mills up on the surface & the occasional jarring thud of someone blasting with black powder somewhere in the mountain. But the miners have not come back down here.

Where could they be? In a town where men work around the clock this place has been empty for what seems like days.

There can only be one explanation.

Walt and his pards have somehow stopped the miners from coming down until they can find me & kill me.

I am hot & damp. I am hungry & I am tired. I am almost out of candles. But at least I have finished this account.

I am so tired I can hardly see straight. So I am going to lie down & have a little rest.

But let the final words of this account be a prayer: 'Lord forgive me for all the things I did wrong in this life. Please bless all those who were kind to me in Satan's Playground & please may Jace not be dead. Lord, grant that I may see You walking on the Streets of Glory. And please may my foster ma & pa & my Indian ma be there, too. Amen.'

WELL YOU HAVE PROBABLY GUESSED THAT I DID not die down there in the deepest shaft of the Mexican Mine, because there are some more sheets with writing on them.

You can also see that the writing is neater & less smudgy than what I wrote when I was down the mine.

That is because I am now writing this at a small table overlooking the 100 mile view in my new lodgings on B Street. It used to be the back room for Bloomfield's Tobacco Emporium. It smells strongly of tobacco and is pretty bare, but it does have that window. I have put in a camp bed & table & chair and it will do for now.

Anyway, here is what happened.

Earlier, when I first found the cavern at the end of that long sloping tunnel, I had an idea. I pulled a strand of wool from the edge of the blanket and I went back along the tunnel a little way. Then I carefully tied that strand of wool at about ankle level between two beams of the frames that shore up the passageway. I figured if Walt or anyone else came close, they would trip & fall & that would alert me to their presence.

I must have dozed off because a man's curse startled me awake. I opened my eyes to Blackness & Heat.

It was darker than a wall of coal painted black. The darkest night you have ever seen was like noonday compared to it. And the heat. I could barely breathe for it. I was slick with sweat.

For a terrible moment I thought I had died & gone to the Fiery Place. Then I smelt the whiskey, urine & alkali water and I remembered where I was. I must have slept longer than I meant to and my candle had burnt out. I reached into my medicine bag for a match & candle. But there was no need. I could now discern a faint yellow glow seeping into my little cavern. The light was increasing, second by second. I deduced from this that someone was coming down the tunnel with a lantern.

I edged round the wall of the cavern and tried to lift the pick as a weapon. But it was too heavy. So I took the hammer. It was pretty heavy, too, but I reckoned I could manage. I scooted as close as I dared to the opening of my cavern. I backed up against the damp rock & prayed that the person with the light was someone who had come to rescue me. The Marshal or a miner. Or maybe even Ping.

The golden lamp-light grew brighter & I could hear footsteps & someone chewing. Even above the smell of alkali water & urine I could smell Bay Rum Hair Tonic. And then the barrel of a big Colt's Army Revolver nosed through the opening like an evil creature poking out of its den. I could not see the owner, just the big gun. It was gripped in a man's left hand. That – and the fact that it had a bone-handled grip – made me certain it was Whittlin Walt.

As the hand with the Colt's Army Revolver nosed its way into my cave, I lifted the heavy hammer back over my head & then I brought it down as hard as I could on the man's wrist.

The gun went off with a noise that nearly deafened me & at the same time the lamp fell & the light went out.

When my ears stopped ringing I could hear a man cursing in language unfit for publication. It was Walt all right. I pulled a match from my medicine pouch & struck it on the rock face. Its bright flare of yellow light showed Walt half-crouched & holding his left wrist, the extinguished oil-lamp rolling on its side, & the Colt's Army Revolver lying almost at my feet.

I blew out the match and – although it was pitch black again – I lunged for the pistol.

I heard Walt's voice only inches away, cursing richly. But I had his piece & I knew the layout of the cave. Holding the revolver in my right hand & using my fingertips on the rock face to guide me, I edged as far away from Walt as I could. Then I transferred the revolver to my left hand, found a match with my right & struck it. The light showed me my last candle on the whiskey crate. I lit it with a trembling hand & then quickly transferred the big pistol to my right hand.

'Dang you, that hurt!' said Walt. He was holding his injured wrist. 'I have been through miles of this danged inferno and I find you in the last place I look. You are slippery-er than a greased weasel. Plus I think you have broke my wrist.'

'Do not move or I will shoot off your kneecaps,' I said, using both hands to train the revolver on him. 'What do you want?'

'You know what I want,' he said. 'I want that Letter.'

'Well, you are not getting it,' I said. 'You can go to Hell. Pardon my French.'

Walt took a step towards me.

I used both thumbs to pull back the stiff hammer of the big Colt. 'Don't think I won't do it.'

'Whoa!' said Walt. He held up his good hand, palm forward. The damaged hand dangled uselessly. 'Don't do anything hasty.' I saw his eyes dart around the cave, like he was looking for a weapon or something to help him.

Then he did something that surprised me.

He smiled.

In the dim light of a single candle I could not tell if it was a Genuine Smile or a Fake Smile.

'I like you, Pinky,' he said through his grinning gritted teeth. 'And I don't want to hurt you.'

I said, 'If you don't want to hurt me, then why were you shooting at me?'

He shrugged & lowered his good hand a little. 'I was

just firing off some warning shots,' he said. 'If I really wanted to hit you I could of. In fact, I have come down here to invite you to join my gang.' He grinned & rubbed the back of his neck with his good hand.

'You want me to join your gang?'

'All you have to do is give me that there Letter,' he said between chomps. 'We will go up to the Recorder's Office together and present that Letter and we will share the proceeds and you can live with me in a big mansion up on A Street. By the end of the year I will have this town in my pocket.'

'Why would you want me in your gang?' I said.

Walt chomped on his tobacco. 'Your ma was a Lakota Squaw named Squats on a Stump. She dropped you behind a bush in a place called Hard Luck, not far from Mount Disappointment. Ain't that so?'

I stared at him. How did he know all those things?

Walt said, 'You think your pa was Robert Pinkerton. But he wasn't.'

The heavy revolver was making my arms ache, but I kept it trained on him. I said, 'Yes, he is. Robert Pinkerton is my pa. He gave me a button off his Pinkerton Rail Road Detective jacket. And he sent my Ma that Letter so we'd be rich.'

'No he didn't,' said Walt. 'That Letter is a clever forgery. I know because I wrote it myself.'

I lowered the revolver but kept it cocked. 'What?' I said.

'Me and your ma concocted that scheme together,'

said Walt. 'But then a band of Shoshone got her and I have been looking for that Letter for a long time. It is a good forgery. It will fool any judge in the Territory.'

'But it was witnessed by my pa, Robert Pinkerton.'

Walt laughed. 'Robert Pinkerton wasn't your pa. And that button isn't his. I won that button off a Pinkerton Rail Road Detective back in '52.'

I felt like someone had punched me in the gut.

I said, 'What are you saying?'

Whittlin Walt smiled at me. 'I am saying that I am your pa.'

LEDGER SHEET 44

I COULD NOT BELIEVE IT.

Whittlin Walt – the most sadistic & hated desperado in the Comstock – was claiming to be my father.

It was so hot & stifling I could not breathe.

I said, 'You are not my pa.' My voice sounded feeble.

Walt said, 'I lied to your ma. I told her I was Robert Pinkerton to impress her. And it worked.'

My heart was thumping. I thought I had Detective Blood flowing in my veins but now it appeared it was Desperado Blood.

'You know that button you got? It came from a jacket I won in a poker game.' He rubbed the back of his neck with his good hand & grinned.

I remembered something Poker Face Jace had told me: One of the signs of an untruthful person is if they rub the back of their neck.

Walt shook his head. 'If you give me that Letter,' he

said, 'then that will prove I can trust you and we can be pardners.'

I remembered something else. Jace told me sometimes people shake their heads when they are saying 'Yes' & sometimes they nod when they are saying 'No'.

Jace told me to believe a person's body, not his words.

A gleam of hope burned in my heart.

I lifted the Colt's Army Revolver again so that it was pointed at his knee. 'Prove you are my pa,' I said. 'Tell me what is my real name. What did my Indian ma call me?'

Walt grinned. In the flickering candle light it made him look evil. 'Your ma named you Glares from a Bush.'

When he said that my knees kind of gave out & I found I was sitting on the upturned bucket I had been using as a chair. I felt sick. I saw some bright little spots, like gnats, swarming across my vision. Maybe I had read him wrong. Maybe he was telling the Truth.

But he had rubbed his neck.

He had shook his head 'No' while meaning 'Yes'.

And he had stopped chewing tobacco just like when he was bluffing at poker.

I had an idea.

I looked up at him. 'You were there when I was born?' I said.

'Course I was,' he said. 'I stayed with your ma a year or two. Then she went her way and I went mine. I always missed not being there to teach you to hunt and fish and shoot.'

'No,' I said. 'No, you are lying. You are not my pa. Here is what happened. You heard from someone that my ma had a valuable Letter from my original pa. I'll bet that someone was Tommy Three. That is probably why he took up with Ma. For riches not love. I never did like him. And I will wager that Letter is real. Otherwise you could just forge another.'

Walt's smile faded & he swallowed hard.

I said, 'They were on their way here. Maybe they were going to meet you. Or maybe only Tommy planned to meet you. But then there was an Indian raid and they died. You tracked me to Temperance and you killed my foster ma & pa and you ransacked the house but you did not find that Letter. You followed me up here to Virginia, and someone told you that I never knew my real pa, so you thought you would pretend to be him. It had to be someone I told my Indian name. It wasn't Tommy Three because ma never told him my Indian name nor hers either. So the traitor must have been someone in Virginia City. I'll bet it was that forked tongue liar Sam Clemens, wasn't it?'

Walt tried to smile but even in the flickering candle light I could tell it was fake. He said, 'I am your real pa. Now give me that Letter, son.'

'I am not your son,' I said. 'If you were really my pa who had held me when I was born, then you would not have called me "son".'

'Why not?'

I said, 'Because I am not a boy. I am a girl.'

241

LEDGER SHEET 45

WALT'S JAW DROPPED OPEN & HE STARED BUG-EYED.
It was the most extreme example of Expression No. 4 I
had ever seen. He had the same expression as a man I
once saw who was kicked by a mule.

'You're a … *girl*?' He said the last word as if it was
something terrible.

'Yes,' I said, lowering the heavy pistol. 'I am a girl.'

Walt said, 'That is impossible. Everybody knows you
are a boy. Tommy Three told me you was. They told me
down in Temperance, too. And even when you dressed
up like a girl you didn't look like one.'

'My Indian ma knew I'd be safer if I pretended to be a boy.
She was the one made me dress like this. But that suited me
fine. And Ma Evangeline agreed it was a good idea.' I took a
step towards him. 'And you just admitted you know Tommy
Three so now I know you are a lying no-good snake.'

He said, 'You ain't no girl. But you ain't like no boy

I ever seen neither. You ain't white and you ain't Injun. You know what you are?' He had Expression No. 3 on his face & he spat on the ground. 'You are a Misfit.'

I looked at him & swallowed hard. 'I may be a Misfit,' I said. 'But I am also P.K. Pinkerton. And now I know what to do.'

I put down his heavy revolver & pulled the Letter out of my medicine bag.

Carefully & deliberately, I tore up the document giving The Bearer the right to half of Virginia City & the Layer of Silver Frosting beneath it. Then I let all the tiny pieces flutter down to my feet.

'No!' yelled Walt. And then he did something I had not been expecting. He reached into his pocket with his good right hand & pulled out a gun. It was my own Smith & Wesson's seven-shooter & he was pointing it straight at me.

This is what I was thinking: 'That Smith & Wesson's seven-shooter can't hit me, but if I could wing him with his Revolver I would not be killing him.'

So I reached for the big, bone-handled Colt.

A gunshot rang out. At the same moment I felt like someone had punched me hard, and I fell to the ground.

Sam Clemens had been wrong.

Apparently you *could* hit something with that Smith & Wesson's seven-shooter.

LEDGER SHEET 46

I FELT A BURNING SENSATION IN MY LEFT SHOULDER & I could smell gunsmoke. I sat up and when I looked down I could see a patch of blood staining the butter-soft buckskin sleeve of my left arm. Then I raised my head up just in time to see Walt pull back the hammer to fire a second shot.

As Walt cocked the gun I scooted back. And he stepped forward.

That was a big mistake.

Do you remember I said that there was a pit above boiling water in the part of the mine where I was hiding? Well, I thought something like this might happen so I had taken away the DANGUR sign and spread out that pale yellow blanket across the open mouth of the pit and then I had sprinkled it all over with dirt to disguise it.

When Walt stepped forward to shoot me a second time, he was not stepping onto solid ground. He was stepping onto a dusty blanket over a mile-deep pit with boiling water at the bottom.

The report of the first shot was still echoing in the small cave and the seven-shooter went off again as his open-mouthed face and upraised hands followed his body rapidly down out of sight. When the second echo died away I could still hear his yell. It was getting fainter and fainter as he dropped down to Hell. Pardon my French.

Clutching my injured left arm, I stood up & went cautiously to the edge of the pit & looked down. I could not see anything, just a deep, black hole such as I never want to see again in my entire life.

Walt was down there somewhere. Maybe he was still falling. Or maybe he was being cooked. The world was well rid of him.

Flickering candlelight showed a glint of metal there in the dust and I saw it was my Smith & Wesson's seven-shooter. It must have flown out of Walt's hand as he dropped down the abyss. I am not sure what Pa Emmet would have said but I offered up a prayer of thanks.

I went around the hole and picked up the pistol. I managed to flip it open with just one hand and to replace the spent charges with fresh cartridges.

At that point I felt sick and had to vomit.

I know I had promised Ma Evangeline I would never drink liquor, but the taste of vomit was sour in my mouth and Walt had knocked over my coffee-pot of alkali water. So I went back to the crate of whiskey & took one of the bottles & smashed the neck & poured some whiskey into the tin can I had been drinking from.

It tasted foul but it revived me and made the throbbing in my left arm more bearable.

I needed to keep my wits about me.

Boz and Extra Dub could be here any moment. But now that I was doubly armed, I could try to make my way back out.

I picked up Walt's Army Revolver, which I had put down on the crate. It was hard to check the cylinder of that big gun with just one hand, but I managed to determine how many charges remained. I also managed to tuck my buckskin shirt into my buckskin pants. Then, making sure Walt's big revolver was between chambers, I stuck it inside my shirt. The gun was hard & bumpy against my chest, so I stuck the ledger sheets down there for padding. Finally I picked up the tin lamp and some other things that had fallen down. I managed to re-light the lamp using just my right hand.

I now had a light that could not easily be extinguished and two firearms. If either of Walt's men appeared, I was prepared. Of course, I had promised my dying ma I would not take a man's life, but I could always shoot them in the legs. That would discourage them from following me.

It is mighty difficult to climb spiral stairs with only one good arm to hold on, especially if you are tired & dizzy & holding a lamp in your teeth with a sheaf of papers & a big gun down your shirt. But after a long time I managed to reach the next level. It was the big gallery. I put down the lamp & rested a little with my back against the great vein of quartz. I was dripping with sweat & blood & candle-grease.

I must have passed out for a moment because something woke me.

It was some rats moving nearby, just outside the circle of lamplight.

And there was another sound: the sound of feet coming down the ladder.

I stood up & nearly passed out again, but after a few breaths I was able to move away from the circle of light cast by my tin lamp.

I hid behind an upright beam, & sure enough I saw another glow of light growing stronger as it descended.

I reached into the neck of my buckskin shirt & pulled out the big Colt's Army Revolver & I took a deep breath & I quietly pulled back the stiff hammer.

'P.K.?' came a familiar voice in a Southern drawl. 'P.K. are you down here?'

I recognized the voice of Poker Face Jace.

'Jace!' I said. 'Is that you? Are you alive?' My voice was real feeble but he heard me. I saw him coming out of the dark towards me. The oil lamp he carried illuminated him from below & it almost looked as if he was smiling. 'Yeah,' he said. 'I'm alive.'

I released the hammer on the revolver & put it back in my shirt. 'I thought Walt's pard shot you,' I said.

'I was saved by Stonewall's quick action,' said Jace,

'and by a pack of cards in my breast pocket. The ball hit me there and knocked me down. Stonewall swears he hit one of Walt's henchmen, but they both got away.' He held his lamp up to my blood-soaked arm. 'But how are you?'

'I am tolerable,' I said. 'Walt winged me with my own seven-shooter but he is burning in Hellfire about now.'

'That is good news,' said Jace. 'Can you hang on to my lamp? I can't hold both you and it.'

I nodded & took his lamp with my good hand.

He swung me up into his arms & carried me back to the bottom of the ladder. He smelled of cigar smoke & coffee. It was a nice smell.

'I've got him!' he yelled up. 'I've got P.K.'

'Do you need help?' The deep voice was Stonewall's, seeming to come from miles above.

'No!' called Jace. 'I can manage.' Then he looked at me. 'Do you mind if I sling you over my shoulder?'

'Go right ahead,' I said.

He started to put me gently over his shoulder but stopped. 'Jesus!' he said. 'What have you got in there?'

'It's Walt's revolver,' I said.

'Better let me take that,' he said. I pulled out the Colt's Army Revolver & gave it to him. He stuck it in his belt & hiked me up. I tried not to cry out from the pain in my arm as he got me settled. I was still holding the lamp in my right hand. As he went up & up, its light showed me how far we would fall if the ladder broke. I clung on & prayed that I would not pass out or be sick again.

When we finally reached the top of the ladder, Stonewall was there with another lamp.

His ugly happy face was a sight to behold.

The blood was whooshing in my ears & my arm was throbbing. I must have passed out for a moment because when I opened my eyes I was no longer upside down. I was in Stonewall's arms & Jace was walking beside us, holding both lamps.

We were in that long dark tunnel, just passing the black pony at her whim. Apart from the three of us & the horse, the mine was still deserted. I could not understand it.

Finally I saw the wonderful yellow glimmer of daylight. At last we emerged into dazzling sunshine & fresh air as welcome to me as a drink of cool water. If I had been strong enough I would have kissed the ground.

I thought, 'I will never go in a tunnel again.'

The light hurt my eyes & I shaded them with my good hand. After a while I could make out a crowd of men standing around.

'There wasn't a cave-in,' called Jace. 'You can all go back to work now.'

'See that there?' growled Stonewall in my ear. He tipped his head towards a sign outside the mine entrance. It read: DO NOT ENTER. CAVE IN.

'Do you mean to say it's all a joke?' said a man in wire-rimmed spectacles. I could see about a hundred whiskered miners all clumped up behind him.

'Yep,' said Jace. 'Whittlin Walt played a bad joke on

you today. But don't you worry. He won't be playing any more jokes, will he P.K.?'

'No, sir,' I said.

Stonewall moved back as the men surged forward & their foreman began barking orders.

As Stonewall carried me away from the entrance of the Mexican Mine, Jace leaned in & said, 'That is why it took us so long to find you. Walt must have put up that sign. All the mine people thought it was real.'

'How did you know I'd be here then?'

Stonewall was carrying me down the mountain, & Jace was walking beside us in long easy strides.

Jace said, 'A lot of people saw Walt chasing you but it was a little girl who lives in a mansion up here on A Street who finally told us. She was looking out her window early Sunday morning & she saw you run into the mouth of the Mexican Mine. She told her pa and he told the Marshal and the Marshal told me. I went down to his office this morning to see if there was any news of you,' he added.

I thought, 'Who could that little girl have been?'

Jace was still talking. 'When we saw Boz & Extra Dub lurking up there on the ridge, we figured Walt was down the mine.'

I said, 'Where are Boz and Extra Dub now?'

Jace said, 'When they saw us coming they got on their horses and vamoosed. There's warrants out on them.'

'How long was I down there?'

'About 30 hours.'

'Only one day? It felt like a week.'

Jace grinned. 'Nope. It's only Monday. Monday lunchtime. What do you say to a cup of black coffee & a piece of cake?'

I said, 'Bee.'

'Beg pardon?' said Jace.

I said, 'Was the little girl's name Bee Bloomfield?'

'I'm not sure,' said Jace, but here she comes. 'You can ask her yourself.'

LEDGER SHEET 47

'So,' said Sam Clemens, as the doctor cut away the buckskin sleeve, 'it appears I was wrong. That little seven-shooter can hit after all.'

'Yes, it can,' I said. 'And it hurts like hell. Pardon my French. Anyhow, I am not talking to you. You are a lying, two-faced Varmint.'

We were in the lean-to annex of the Territorial Enterprise on A Street. Sam Clemens had been going to investigate the alleged 'Cave-In' and had seen me with Jace & Stonewall & Bee Bloomfield. He told them to bring me there & he sent Horace the Printer's Devil to fetch a doctor.

I was lying on one of the bunk beds on crumpled sheets. Jace & Stonewall and some newspapermen were crowded around me as the doctor examined my arm. Bee Bloomfield was there too. She was holding the pan for the doctor.

'Why do you call me a lying, two-faced Varmint?' said Sam Clemens. 'I confess I can be two-faced and I have also been known to lie, but why a Varmint?'

I said, 'Because you told Whittlin Walt my real Indian name and all sorts of other things.'

Sam Clemens said, 'He threatened to take off one of my ears if I did not give him some information about you. I figured your Injun name was the least harmful thing I could tell him.'

'It was not the least harmful thing you could have told him,' I said to Sam Clemens. 'Whittlin Walt pretended to be my pa. And because he knew my Indian name, he almost convinced me.'

'What is your Indian name?' asked Poker Face Jace. 'I would like to know.'

Sam Clemens opened his mouth but I said, 'Don't you dare tell.'

'Swallow this,' said the doctor, handing me a glass with a few inches of pale yellow liquid. He was a white-haired man with oval spectacles.

'What is it?'

'Laudanum. It will kill the pain while I probe for the ball.'

The doctor lifted my head & Bee brought the glass to my mouth & helped me drink it down. It tasted strange & made my mouth tingle.

'How did you figure out Walt was lying?' said Poker Face Jace.

I lay back on a pillow. 'He rubbed the back of his neck

& he shook his head,' I said. 'But the real giveaway was when he stopped chewing his tobacco. That's when I knew he was bluffing.'

'Bravo,' said Jace. 'You are a fast learner. It took me an hour to figure that out.'

'I am a good liar,' remarked Sam Clemens. 'I made sixteen hay wagons where there was only one. But I am not a Varmint.'

I felt kind of warm & floating. 'You have strange ears,' I said to Sam Clemens. 'They have no lobes.'

'What about my ears,' said Bee, pushing back her curls and turning her head.

'They are real whirly,' I said.

'I think the laudanum is taking effect,' said the doctor. 'I'll have a look for that ball now.' He smiled at me. 'So, young man, I gather your name is Pinkerton, like mine.'

'You are called Pinkerton?' I said.

'I am. Doctor Thomas H. Pinkerton. You a relative of the Chicago Pinkertons?'

'I thought I was,' I said. 'But now I am not sure.'

I felt sick. But it might have been because Doc Pinkerton was fishing around in my arm for a metal ball.

'Do not be cast down,' said Sam Clemens. 'You ain't the first and you won't be the last not to know who your pa is.'

'One thing I do know,' I said, 'is that I *feel* like a Pinkerton. I mean, I like solving mysteries and figuring out how things work. And I kind of like Disguises, too.'

'Eureka,' said the doctor. 'He held up a pea-sized ball between the prongs of his tweezers. 'Here is the culprit. A .22 ball.'

'Ball like a homeopathic pill,' said Sam Clemens. 'It would take a bigger dose than that to kill Pinky here. Still, maybe I should take back my seven-shooter.'

'Please may I keep it?' I said. 'Even though it shot me?' I looked at Sam Clemens. 'I hope you don't write about this,' I said. 'If you do, then Walt's men might come back and take revenge.'

He sighed a deep sigh. 'Yes, you may keep that gun and no, I will not write about it.' Then he lowered his voice and brought his head close. 'I have just had an idea of an Indian massacre based on your story,' he whispered. 'I will use that instead. With your permission.'

'You are welcome to it,' I said.

From across the room a voice said, 'Poker Face Jace may believe in twitches and ticks, but I am not convinced. Are you sure Walt was not your pa?' It was the young man with the plug hat & walking stick who had been drinking with Sam Clemens.

'That is Mr. Joe Goodman,' said Sam under his breath. 'Owner of the Territorial Enterprise and my boss.'

'I am sure Walt was not my pa,' I said. 'I got him to admit it.'

'How?' said several people at once.

'Simple,' I said. 'I told him I was really a girl and not a boy. And that if he was really my pa he would have known that. That flummoxed him and he started babbling.'

They all stared at me. They looked pretty flummoxed themselves. Sam Clemens's pipe had fallen out of his mouth.

Jace glanced around at them and rubbed the back of his neck. 'But you were just joshing, weren't you, P.K.? It was just a Bluff to get him to Show His Hand, wasn't it?'

'Yes,' I said. I felt all warm & floaty. 'It was a Bluff to get him to Show His Hand. And it worked.'

LEDGER SHEET 48

THE NEXT AFTERNOON I FINALLY MADE IT TO THE Recorder's Office across the street from the Territorial Enterprise. I was dressed in a mixture of Indian, miner & tony boy get-up. To replace my bloody buckskin shirt, Isaiah Coffin had given me a soft & faded flannel shirt that had once been red, plus a dark blue jacket with brass buttons. I wore my own fringed buckskin pants & my soft buckskin moccasins & the black slouch hat with the hawk feather that Jace had given me. And of course I had my medicine bag, tucked out of sight.

I had been to the Notary Public on B Street. They had stamped something for me & I had bought it over to the Recorder's Office on A Street. Word must have got around because by the time I got to the Recorder's Office I was trailing a group of interested spectators & friends, including Dan De Quille, just back from Carson City & mighty relieved to be in one piece.

There were already two dozen men in the Recorder's Office, bushy & bearded, dusty & lousy, all clamoring to record their claims, but when they saw me with my left arm in a sling they parted like the Red Sea before Moses.

'There he is!' said one in a thick Cornish accent. 'The boy who kilt Whittlin Walt.'

'Heard he shot him between the eyes with a Smith & Wesson's seven-shooter,' said another.

'I heard he wrassled him down to the ground, then tossed him into a bottomless pit full of boiling water.'

'Whittlin Walt is probably still falling,' said a third beard, rubbing the palms of his hands together.

'How can a pit be bottomless and have boiling water in it, too?' asked the first miner.

'Good morning, young man,' said the man behind the counter. He had bushy ginger eyebrows & a mustache like two foxes' tails hanging down either side of his nose. A sign on the desk told me that he was: MR RUFUS E. ARICK, RECORDER. 'Do you have a claim to register?'

'Not exactly, sir,' I said. I handed him the piece of paper in my hand. 'But I have this.'

Mr. Rufus E. Arick frowned at it. 'This is a WANTED poster,' he said. 'For Walt Darmitage – alias Whittlin Walt – wanted in four states and territories for murder, theft and torture. It says REWARD $2000.' He looked at me. 'To collect your reward you must go to see the Marshal. Who's next?'

'Wait,' I said. 'Turn it over.'

'What?'

'Look on the back of the WANTED poster.'

Mr. Rufus E. Arick turned the piece of paper over. There on the back I had glued together all the little scraps of the Letter I had tore up. I had found all the pieces but one and that one was near the top, in an unimportant part of the document. There were some blood spots on them but you could still read the writing.

He looked at the glued-together Letter. Then he looked at me. Then he looked back at the glued-together Letter.

'Son, is this what you have to give me? I am not certain this is a legal document.'

'Look right there,' I said. 'It is signed & witnessed. Signed by Ethan Allen Grosh & witnessed by Robert Pinkerton in November 1857.'

Rufus E. Arick shook his head slowly. 'Even if it *is* legal, so much time has elapsed: nearly five years. You'd certainly have to take it to court. Legal battle like this could last months. They will fight you to the bitter end.'

I said, 'Who is "they"?'

'Why, half the mine owners in Virginia City. This letter threatens them all. The only people who will get rich off this are the Lawyers.'

I felt my heart sink down to my moccasins. Had I risked my life for nothing?

'Never mind, little pard,' said one of the bushy miners. 'That's life on the Comstock. Bonanza one day and borrasca the next.'

'I will buy that Letter,' said a voice from the doorway.

259

LEDGER SHEET 49

EVERYBODY IN THE RECORDER'S OFFICE TURNED.

The man in the doorway wore a black frock coat & gray trowsers. He was blond & clean-shaven, apart from fluffy side whiskers. 'My name is Billy Chollar,' he said, 'and I own the Chollar Mine.'

'The Chollar Mine,' said Dan De Quille under his breath, 'is a hundred feet of the Comstock Ledge a little south of here, not far from the Divide.'

Billy Chollar said, 'My attorney is Mr. William Morris Stewart. He advised me to buy that Letter of yours. He is currently representing me in a big case and says I don't need another. Therefore I propose giving you a couple of feet of my mine. It will pay out a dividend of at least $100 a month. Even in Virginia that is enough to live well.'

I said, 'My dead pa says all Lawyers are the Devil's Own.'

Billy Chollar took a step forward & removed his hat. He had little pouches under his eyes that made him look tired. 'You would have to overcome your prejudice and hire a Lawyer,' he said, 'if you wanted to win that claim. And he'd have to be a good one, too. You'd have to take me and the other Mine Owners to court. You might end up the richest soul on the Comstock, in ten or twelve years. Or you might end up in debt.' Billy sighed & stared at the floor. 'I wish now I had settled with the Potosi Mining Company. The way things are going, my own case against them will take years.' He raised his tired blue eyes and gave me a direct look. 'I am making you a generous offer.'

I studied his feet. They were pointed towards me. His shoulders were relaxed & his hands were holding his hat. He showed no signs of bluffing. I glanced over at Jace. He blew some smoke up & gave me a small nod.

I seemed to hear the voice of my dead foster pa Emmet and I said out loud, 'The love of money is the root of all evil.'

Behind me I heard the familiar drawl of Sam Clemens, 'The *lack* of money is the root of all evil.'

Then a wild-eyed prospector put his bushy face close to mine. 'That Billy Chollar must want it bad, little pard. Go for the riches! Hire a good Lawyer and fight for what's yours.'

That decided me.

'Thank you Mr. Chollar,' I said. 'I accept your kind offer.'

Some people groaned & others applauded. A few hats went up into the air.

Billy Chollar stepped forward & extended his right hand. 'A wise decision,' he said. 'It is hard to resist Greed in this place. Let us shake on it.'

We shook hands. His grip was firm & dry. He was

giving me a Genuine Smile.

'What about the WANTED notice on the back?' said Dan De Quille. 'P.K. should get $2000 for that.'

Billy Chollar replaced his hat on his head. 'I would be happy to take you to the Marshal's Office right now. Once you have collected the reward you can give me the WANTED poster with the deed stuck to the back. Then afterwards you can come over to my Mine Office and we will discuss your "feet" over a cup of coffee. I have a buggy waiting outside.'

I stared at him.

'As a gesture of goodwill,' he said, 'here is two hundred dollars in gold.' He reached into his frock coat & pulled out a leather pouch & counted out ten gold coins.

He held them out to me.

I hesitated.

Dan De Quille said, 'I think you can trust him, P.K. Besides, you have nearly fifty witnesses here, including some influential reporters.'

I took the coins & slipped them into my medicine bag. $200 felt heavy. It felt good.

'Oh, P.K.!' cried a female voice. 'Now you will have enough to go to Chicago and be a Pinkerton Detective and live in Style.'

I turned to see a pretty lady in blue on the arm of Isaiah Coffin, who was pushing through the crowd of beards.

I could not believe my eyes.

It was Belle Donne.

LEDGER SHEET 50

PK PINKERTON
PRIVATE EYE

"WE HARDLY EVER SLEEP"

I PULLED MY SMITH & WESSON FROM MY POCKET and cocked it and drew down on her.

'Oh, P.K.,' she said with a laugh. 'Don't be foolish. Isaiah and I are going to be married. And we have you to thank! If you hadn't tied us together . . . '

Without lowering my gun I looked at Isaiah Coffin. 'Don't trust her,' I said.

'Too late,' he replied. 'I am smitten.'

'And I,' said Titus Jepson, 'am bereft.' He was nursing a heavily bandaged left hand.

Belle kissed Titus on the cheek. 'I am sorry, Dear Titus,' she said. 'But I am going to become an Actress at that new Melodeon when it opens. Isaiah knows the owner and has promised to introduce me. One day I might even perform in San Francisco or Boston or even Chicago.' She looked at me. 'Maybe I will see you there.'

I released the hammer on my pistol and stuck it back in my pocket. 'I am not going to Chicago,' I said.

'London?' said Isaiah Coffin. 'You can afford it now.'

'I reckon not.'

'San Francisco?' said Grafton T. Brown. He had his sketching pad under his left arm.

'Nope.'

'If you stay here in Virginia,' said Titus Jepson. 'I will give you discounted meals till the end of time. You can have cake for breakfast every day,' he said. And then he added, 'As long as you have a square meal for dinner.'

I glanced over at Jace. He winked at me.

I said, 'I have already decided to stay here a few more years.'

I did not tell them my reasoning, but it was this: If I could show my pa Robert Pinkerton that I was a good Detective, maybe he would be proud of me. Maybe he would even let me come and work with him at the Pinkerton Detective Agency in Chicago.

But in the meantime, I figured the best place for me to learn the craft of being a Detective was right here in Virginia.

'Yes,' I repeated, half to myself. 'I believe I will stay right here.'

'Give him three cheers and tiger!' cried Titus Jepson.

Everybody said, 'Hi! Hi! Hi! Hurraaaah!'

'Will you start speculating like the rest of us?' said Dan De Quille, when the roar died down.

'No,' I said. 'I am going to set up my own business.'

'I am Miss Prudence Feather, from the First Ward School,' said a woman's voice. 'And I think you should be in school.'

It was the woman in black from the Colombo Restaurant.

'I tried school once,' I said. 'It was down in Dayton and the bullies impeded me. I can read and write and do math. As far as the rest is concerned, I believe I can educate myself.'

'Quite right,' said Sam Clemens, puffing his rancid pipe. 'I never let school interfere with my education. I started working at the age of thirteen.'

'And I was only twelve,' said Dan De Quille.

'I will teach you ancient Chinese art of fighting,' said an accented voice. I turned to see Ping pushing his way through the crowd. 'After you pay me what you owe me: five hundred dollar,' he added.

I nodded at him. I meant to keep my promise.

'The Martial Arts are always useful,' said Isaiah Coffin. 'But if you wish to broaden your understanding of human nature and great literature, you should borrow some of my Shakespeare plays. I have them all.'

'I can teach you a few useful Latin phrases,' said Joe Goodman.

Miss Feather harrumphed. 'What about arithmetic?'

Poker Face Jace removed his cigar & examined it. 'I do not mean to be rude, Ma'am,' he said. 'But P.K. is probably better at adding & subtracting and all those other things than anybody in this room, including you.' He sucked on his cigar & then blew the smoke up high. 'P.K.?' he said. 'Tell this lady how many cubic feet of space a mine would have if it has four miles of tunnel eight foot wide and eight foot high.'

'Let's see,' I said. 'A mile is 5,280 feet so that would make 1,351,680 cubic feet.'

Over at his desk Mr. Rufus E. Arick made a quick calculation on a sheet of paper. Then he looked up with a number 4 expression all over his face. 'He's right.'

Most everybody cheered. Miss Feather snorted. 'Besides,' I said, 'I want to learn what they do not teach you at school. I want to learn how to understand people.' I looked at Poker Face Jace. 'Not all the best teachers are in school.'

Poker Face Jace winked at me but Miss Feather was not convinced by my argument.

She said, 'Harrumph.' Then she turned on her heel & exited the room.

'You say you intend to set up a business?' said Dan De Quille. 'Here in Virginia?'

'Yes, sir,' I said. 'I am going to ask Mr. Sol Bloomfield if he will let me rent or buy his small shop space on B Street, the one between Mr. Isaiah Coffin's Ambrotype & Photographic Gallery & the Colombo Restaurant. I will make it my place of residence as well as my office.'

'Why son,' said one of the prospectors. 'With $100 a month you will never have to work in your life.'

'Hundred a month is as much as I earn,' said Sam

Clemens, puffing on his pipe. 'And you don't even have to lift a finger. Just waltz down to the mine office & collect your gold.'

'Yeah,' said another bearded prospector. 'That's the dream of most of us: to retire & never work again.'

'But I want to work,' I said. 'I want to go into business.'

'Quite right, too,' said Dan De Quille. 'A person should not be idle. What kind of business are you considering?'

I took my Pinkerton Rail Road Detective Button from my pocket & looked at it.

Then I said, 'I am going into the Detective Business. It is my Destiny.'

Almost everybody laughed, as if this was a fine joke.

'No Rail Road here yet,' said Dan De Quille.

'Will you work for one of the stagecoach companies?' asked Titus Jepson.

'Or the Marshal?' said Isaiah Coffin.

'No,' I said. 'I am going to work for myself. I will help people by Solving Crimes. If they are happy with the result they can pay me.'

'That might work in Chicago,' said Isaiah Coffin, 'but I doubt you'll make a success of it here. I suggest you open a Dry Goods store.'

'Or a tobacconist,' said Dan De Quille with a glance at Sam Clemens. 'We need more purveyors of good tobacco here in Virginia.'

'Just don't start a rival newspaper,' said Joe Goodman.

Jace said, 'I still think you should come work for me.'

'I will be happy to help you some evenings,' I said to

Jace. 'But I am set on being a Detective and my own boss.'

'You know,' said Sam Clemens, as he lit his pipe, 'they say when Satan was panning for sinners they all ended up here.'

'Speak for yourself!' said a bearded miner & everybody laughed.

Sam Clemens ignored him. 'I am just saying: if P.K. wants to go into the Detective business, he will never be short of work.'

'I think it is a good idea,' said Mr. Billy Chollar. 'There are some people here I'd like to know more about.'

'And I think my pard is cheating me,' said a beard, 'but I can't figure out how. I'd employ you to follow him & find out.'

'They call that "shadowing", I believe,' said Belle Donne. 'It sounds real exciting. You know,' she added. 'I lost a ruby necklace a while back and I would hire you to find it.'

'And I need some good Scoops,' said Sam Clemens. 'Ones I can publish. I'd pay a dollar or two for some promising leads.'

Dan De Quille shook his head. 'I am still skeptical,' he said. 'But I wish you good luck.'

Titus Jepson said, 'Which of those cases will you take first?'

I said, 'I will take them all. But first I will ask Mr. Grafton T. Brown here if he will paint me a shingle for my office.'

Grafton T. Brown gave a nod of his head & said, 'It will be a pleasure. What would you like your shingle to say?'

I pondered for a moment & then I said, 'P.K. Pinkerton, Private Eye. We Hardly Ever Sleep.'

At that everybody cheered & some of them lifted me up on their shoulders & they carried me out into the bright September sunshine to Billy Chollar's buggy.

As a rule, I do not like to be touched.

But this time I did not mind.

The sky was blue & the sun was warm. Somewhere in a sage bush a quail called out, 'Chicago! Chicago!'

I thought, 'Not yet. I am staying here a little longer.'

The mine whistles were shrilling noon & the Washoe Canaries were braying & in a saloon a hurdy gurdy was churning out 'Camptown Races'.

And beneath it all I could hear the thump of the mountain, like the heartbeat of God.

Read on for the Glossary and a sneak preview of P.K.'s next exciting adventure . . .

GLOSSARY

ALKALI – a harsh chemical found in both dust and water in parts of Nevada.

AMBROTYPE – one of the earliest types of photograph, invented in the 1850s.

ASSAY OFFICE – a place you could take your sample of ore to see how much it was worth.

BONANZA – a sudden dramatic increase in wealth, especially when mining.

BORRASCA – the opposite of bonanza, i.e. a worthless mine or claim.

CALIBER – the diameter of balls and bullets measured in hundredths of an inch.

CELESTIAL – slang for Chinese because the imperial court in China was known as the 'celestial court'.

COMSTOCK – the ledge of silver below

Virginia City was known as the Comstock Lode after one of the original stakeholders. The whole region was sometimes called the Comstock.

CREESUS – a misspelling of Croesus: a mythical king who was fabulously wealthy.

CRIB – a square structure like a manger, the framework of a mine or a one-room dwelling.

DAN DE QUILLE – the pen name of Virginia City journalist William Wright.

DERINGER OR DERRINGER – a small one- or two-shot pistol with big bullets that was easy to hide.

DRAW A BEAD ON/DRAW DOWN ON – expressions which meant to point a gun at someone.

GRAFTON T. BROWN – a freeborn African American artist best known for his city views.

GROSH BROTHERS – Hosea and Ethan probably discovered the silver lode beneath Virginia City but died before they could benefit.

HOOP SKIRT – a skirt worn over petticoats with hoops sewn in.

HURDY GIRLS – women who worked in saloons where music was often played on a hurdy gurdy (a hand-cranked stringed soundbox).

LAKOTA – (a.k.a. Sioux) the language and name of a Native American people from South Dakota.

LEDGE – An underground layer of valuable ore.

Mark Twain – one of America's most famous writers; his real name was Sam Clemens.

medicine bag – a pouch carried by some Native Americans, usually for magical purposes.

mother lode – a mining term which means the main vein or ledge of ore.

Mount Davidson – the Comstock Lode was in it and Virginia City upon it.

notary public – a person authorized to draw up documents and/or certify them as legal.

ore – earth or rock containing valuable metal or mineral.

passel – a large group of people or things.

Pinkerton Detective Agency – founded by Allan Pinkerton in Chicago in 1850.

Paiute – the Northern Paiute were a tribe of Native Americans who lived in Nevada, Oregon and parts of California.

placer mining – where surface deposits of earth are rinsed with water to reveal gold.

plug – a bowler hat, a piece of chewing tobacco, or an old horse.

Potosi – a claim in Virginia City named after a silver-rich mountain in Bolivia.

quartz stamp mill – a machine with pistons that pulverized rock in order to remove metal.

recorder's office – the place where official records concerning property or mining claims were kept.

SAM CLEMENS – (see Mark Twain) was a reporter for the Daily Territorial Enterprise from 1862 to 1864.

SLOUCH HAT – a soft felt hat with a wide flexible brim, usually in brown or black.

SOILED DOVE – a term used to describe a woman who worked in a saloon or brothel.

SPITTOON – a metal container to catch people's saliva when they chewed tobacco and spat out the juice.

STAKING A CLAIM – the act of physically marking the place where you intended to mine.

STOVEPIPE HAT – a tall cylindrical hat, famously worn by President Abraham Lincoln.

TAILINGS – ore was crushed in stamp mills to extract precious metal; the left-over piles of pulverized earth were called tailings.

TEAMSTER – the driver of a team of animals, usually oxen or mules.

TERRITORIAL ENTERPRISE (A.K.A. DAILY TERRITORIAL ENTERPRISE) – the first daily newspaper published in Virginia City from 1860 on.

TONY BUNCH – slang for a group of 'high-tone' or wealthy people.

VIRGINIA CITY – a mining town in Nevada that sprang up in 1859, soon after silver was discovered.

WASHOE – the name of a lake to the west of Virginia City and the area around it, and also of a Native American people of that region.

WASHOE CANARY – an ironic slang term for a braying mule in Virginia City.

WASHOE ZEPHYR – an ironic slang term for the violent wind in Virginia City.

WELLS FARGO – Wells, Fargo & Co. was founded in 1848 to transport and bank money, payrolls and gold.

WHANG LEATHER – tough strips of leather used for thongs, reins and harnesses.

WHIM – a wheel-like mechanism for raising ore or water from a mine.

P.K. PINKERTON IS BACK AND ON
THE TRAIL OF A MURDERER IN

THE CASE OF THE
GOOD-LOOKING CORPSE

AVAILABLE NOW!

READ ON FOR A SPECIAL PREVIEW . . .

LEDGER SHEET 1

MY NAME IS P.K. PINKERTON & I AM A PRIVATE
Eye operating out of Virginia City, Nevada Territory. At
the moment I am in Jail on the charge of Murder.

I am writing this Journal because my lawyer told me
to set down my side of the story. He told me to write it
as if I was talking to a jury of '12 good men and true'
or a kindly sympathetic Judge with 'white hair and
twinkling eyes'.

He said I should start by putting my name, age &
qualifications.

I have already stated my name: P.K. Pinkerton.

I am 12 years old.

I can read & write & I can speak American and
Lakota. I can also speak a little Spanish & Chinese & a
few words of French.

I am real good at tracking & hunting. My eyes are as
sharp as a hawk's & my ears are as keen as a rabbit's &

279

my sense of smell is almost as good as a bear's.

For the sake of honesty, I must confess that I have a Thorn.

My Thorn is that people confound me. I am not good at reading people's faces & sometimes have trouble knowing if they are telling the truth or lying.

As well as my Thorn, I have some Foibles & Eccentricities.

One of my Foibles is that I get the Mulligrubs.

One of my Eccentricities is I like Collecting things.

It is my Foibles & Eccentricities – and my Thorn – that have landed me here in jail today, beneath the shadow of the hangman's noose.

LEDGER SHEET 2

HERE IS WHAT HAPPENED.

After vanquishing three Deadly Desperados last Monday, I used $300 of the Reward Money to buy premises for my new business.

Mr. Sol Bloomfield was in the process of amalgamating his two small Tobacco Stores into one big Emporium down on C Street. I bought the smallest of his stores, the one on South B Street. Although it is long & narrow it suits me fine because it is located next to a Photographic Studio (where I can get disguises) and the Colombo Restaurant (where I take my meals).

Mr. Bloomfield removed the last of his cigars & snuff & pipe tobacco from that store on Tuesday evening at 5.00 pm.

I moved in on Tuesday evening at 6.00 pm.

I opened my door for business at 9.00 am on Weds 1 October.

I had put up a shingle outside my front door with the words: *P.K. Pinkerton, Private Eye. We Hardly Ever Sleep.* And I had a big sign in the window of the door that told people I was OPEN.

I had been greatly supported by the townsfolk after vanquishing a deadly desperado a few days before, and I was confident that I would soon get many clients. My foster pa Emmet always used to tell me to 'strike while the iron is hot'.

But all that morning not a single person came in through my door.

Maybe it was because the Washoe Zephyr had been blowing hard since the night before. I had been finishing the account of my first Case and did not notice but now that I had nothing to do but sit and wait for clients, the powerful wind seemed to taunt me. They call it a 'zephyr' but it was howling & moaning & spitting gravel at my shop front. My left arm began to throb where I had been shot two days before by a .22 caliber ball.

I began to feel very low.

By and by I felt so low that I was in danger of getting the Mulligrubs.

'The Mulligrubs' is what my Foster Ma Evangeline called a bad kind of trance that creeps up on me when I feel low. I can stay in those Bad Trances for hours. I rock & moan & cannot easily be roused. When I come out of those trances, my brain feels thick & wooly, as if my head was stuffed full of cotton balls. Getting the Mulligrubs is another one of my Foibles.

Ma Evangeline – God rest her soul – taught me a way of staving off the Mulligrubs. If I concentrate on ordering a Collection it distracts me & I forget to be low. When I was living with Ma Evangeline and Pa Emmet down in Temperance, they let me keep a Bug Collection & a Button Collection.

But I did not have either of those collections at my new residence in Virginia City, so I looked about me with an aim to starting a new one.

Mr. Sol Bloomfield had left all the labels on the shelves along with the tobacco crumbs & flakes that gave the place its distinctive smell.

I went back to my desk & found a pack of cigarrito papers & spread them out & copied down the names of all the different tobaccos. Then I went to the shelves and found bits of tobacco & started to put a sample of each tobacco on top of every label.

Using an out-of-date brochure that Mr. Bloomfield left behind, I catalogued over 50 Cuban Cigars, 32 Domestic Cigars, 17 types of Leaf Tobacco, 12 different Plugs & Twists and 6 varieties of Snuff.

So that made over 100 types of smoking, chewing and leaf tobacco. I decided to call it my Big Tobacco Collection so that it would begin with 'B' like my other 2 collections: Bugs & Buttons.

Sometimes I looked up at the door that still admitted no Clients & I felt kind of queasy in my stomach. But as soon as I returned to my new task I felt better.

In this way I staved off the Mulligrubs & fought

the urge to be downcast. Sometimes I even forgot my throbbing arm & the howling wind & the memory of the terrible thing I had seen in my cabin down in Temperance.

It was a little past 5pm and the sun had just dipped behind Mount Davidson, when a bearded miner flung open the door to my office. I was so absorbed in ordering flecks of snuff that I almost jumped out of my skin. Some of that Zephyr whirled in and threatened to stir up my Big Tobacco Collection, so I shielded it with my arms & asked the man to shut the door.

He did so & stood there panting.

As I said, I am not good at reading people. It is my Thorn.

Ma Evangeline taught me 5 facial Expressions to look out for.

No. 1 - If someone's mouth curves up & their eyes crinkle, that is a Genuine Smile.

No. 2 - If their mouth stretches sideways & their eyes are not crinkled, that is a Fake Smile.

No. 3 - If a person turns down their mouth & crinkles up their nose, they are disgusted.

No. 4 - If their eyes open real wide, they are probably surprised or scared.

No. 5 - If they make their eyes narrow, they are either mad at you or thinking or suspicious.

The eyes of the miner who had just burst into my office were open real wide.

It was definitely Expression No. 4.

He was scared.

I thought, 'At last. Someone has brought me a mystery to solve.'

LEDGER SHEET 3

'ARE YOU THE DETECTIVE?' CRIED THE BEARDED miner, taking a step into my narrow office.

I did not betray my excitement at receiving my first Client.

'Yes,' I said in a calm & businesslike tone. 'I am P.K. Pinkerton, Private Eye. No problem too big, no case too small.'

'Come quick!' panted the miner. 'It's gone! It was thar a minute ago and now it's gone! Come see!'

I got up & grabbed my good slouch hat from a peg by the door & flipped my OPEN sign to CLOSED & followed him outside, closing the door as quickly as I could. Out on the blustery boardwalk, the shrieking Zephyr tried to snatch the hat from my head & the blue woolen coat from my back. Two other men were standing out there on the boardwalk. The wind was whipping up their slouch hats, beards & flannel shirts, and even the pants tucked into knee-high boots. I deduced from their flapping attire that they were miners, too.

As I locked the door behind me, they were all crying, 'It's gone! It's gone!'

'What is gone?' I asked the miners. I had to shout to make myself heard.

'Come on,' said the first one. 'We'll show you!'

The 3 miners led the way: north along B Street & then left up Sutton towards A Street, their long brown beards fluttering behind them like pennants.

The wind was so strong that it made the planks of the boardwalk rattle. We had to lean into it at an angle of about 45 degrees just to make headway. That blasting Zephyr had driven most people indoors but a passing woman screamed as it lifted her hoop skirt right over her head to reveal frilly bloomers. A small dog was being pushed down the street in the opposite direction to the one it was heading. Oxen and mules kept their heads down & their eyes squinched & their teeth gritted.

In front of me, the three miners were shouting things like, 'Where d'you think it went?' and 'Who could of took it?'

'What is gone?' I repeated into the howling wind.

'Thar!' shouted the first miner, pointing. 'It was right thar!'

I stopped and stared at the northwest corner of Sutton and A Street. I could not believe my eyes. Through a cloud of dust I could see nothing but a Vacant Lot.

'The Daily Territorial Enterprise Newspaper building,' I said. 'It is gone.'

Two days previously I had been carried to the reporters' sleeping area next to the newspaper's printing office so that I could have a .22 caliber bullet dug out of my arm. Now the wooden building & its lean-to annex had Completely Vanished.

There remained not a single stick of wood. A tumbleweed sped across that Vacant Lot; it was going about a mile a minute.

'It was thar yesterday,' Miner No. 2 shouted above the howling wind.

'And now it's gone,' shouted Miner No. 3.

'Who could of took it?' shouted the first miner. 'You're a Detective. You better look for clews!'

I looked around.

A woman's parasol flew by.

'Lookee here,' shouted Miner No. 2. 'There might be a clew in this morning's paper.' He held it out.

The half-folded newspaper was flapping in the violent wind so I took it & looked where his grubby finger was stabbing & I read the following:

A GALE. About 7 o'clock Tuesday evening a sudden blast of wind picked up a shooting gallery, two lodging houses and a drug store from their tall wooden stilts and set them down again some ten or twelve feet back of their original location, with such a degree of roughness as to jostle their insides into a sort of chaos. There were many guests in the lodging houses at the time of the accident, but it is pleasant to reflect that they seized their carpet sacks and vacated the premises. No one hurt.

'Do you think maybe it was the Washoe Zephyr?' said the first miner above the howling wind. 'Do you think this pesky breeze lifted it right up and set it down elsewheres?'

'That thar wind is a *Scriptural Wind*,' shouted another, 'on account of no man knows *whence it cometh*.'

I looked down at the article & then back up to find the three miners laughing & slapping their thighs & pointing at me.

'He believed us!' cried one.

'He was looking for clews!' shouted another.

'He calls himself a "Detective"!' laughed the third.

That was when I realized the Ugly Truth.

They had not brought me my first case. They were pranking me.

I clenched my fists and considered kicking the nearest miner hard in the shin. But Pa Emmett had taught me not to kick people hard in the shin. He taught me to count to ten & quote Philippians 4:5, *'Let your moderation be known to all men.'*

So I did not kick any of the miners hard in the shin. Nor did I draw down on them with the Smith & Wesson's seven-shooter in my pocket.

Instead I took a deep breath & bowed my head & counted to ten & quoted Philippians 4:5.

'Amen,' I said.

As I lifted my head, the wind seemed to die down a

little. I saw that the miners had gone & a tall man in a flapping gray suit stood beside me. He had a round face, a dark mustache & clean-shaven chin. He was smoking a cigar. He looked familiar.

'Hello, P.K.,' he shouted above the wind. 'Are you looking for the Enterprise?'

'Yes,' I shouted back. 'Some miners told me this wind blew it away. I reckon they were pranking me.'

'Yes, indeed,' he shouted. 'We moved down to our fine new premises on C Street yesterday. I guess those Chinese firewood-peddlers have been over this place and picked it clean.' He sucked his cigar & blew out & the wind snatched away the smoke. 'I came up here to see what still needed doing, but the answer is nary a thing. I could not have hired men to do such a good job.'

I pointed at the article in the fluttering newspaper. 'They tried to use this article called *A GALE* to convince me,' I said.

The man leant forward and looked at the article.

'Oh, that is just an attempt at humor by Mr. Sam Clemens, our new Local Reporter,' he said. 'He is still finding his feet, as they say.'

Then I recognized the man who was speaking to me. He was Mr. Joe Goodman, one of the co-owners of the Daily Territorial Enterprise Newspaper. He had promised to teach me some Latin phrases.

'You promised to teach some Latin phrases,' I said.

'So I did,' he replied. 'Why don't you come down and visit us one day? You can find us at 27 North C Street.'

'I will.' I folded the newspaper & put it in my coat pocket & turned to go back to my office.

'Oh, P.K.?' he said, shouting against the wind.

I turned back. 'Yes?'

'Do not be discouraged. *Fortes fortuna iuvat.*'

'Beg pardon?'

He took out a pencil and wrote it down on the margin of my newspaper.

'That is Latin,' he said, 'It means "Fortune favors the brave".'

CAROLINE LAWRENCE

Caroline Lawrence is American. She grew up in Bakersfield, California and claims that some of her ancestors were pioneers, teamsters & newspapermen. Caroline came to England to study Classics at Cambridge. After a decade of immersing herself in Roman history in order to write *The Roman Mysteries*, Caroline is now mining the rich vein of American history during the tumultuous 1860s. She lives in London by the river with her history-loving husband Richard, who did the illustrations inside this book.

The P.K. Pinkerton Mysteries is an action-packed historical fiction series where a unique hero interacts with real historical characters and events.

Choose one of the twin portals on Caroline's website
www.carolinelawrence.com to enter
The Wild West www.pkpinkerton.com
Ancient Rome www.romanmysteries.com